Enjoy your book

best wi

Elizabeth

THE LYON AND THE LAMB

The Lyon's Den Connected World

Elizabeth Keysian

Text by Elizabeth Keysian
Cover by Dar Albert

Dragonblade Publishing, Inc. is an imprint of Kathryn Le Veque Novels, Inc.
P.O. Box 23
Moreno Valley, CA 92556
ceo@dragonbladepublishing.com

Produced in the United States of America

First Edition May 2023
Print Edition

ARE YOU SIGNED UP FOR DRAGONBLADE'S BLOG?

You'll get the latest news and information on exclusive giveaways, exclusive excerpts, coming releases, sales, free books, cover reveals and more.

Check out our complete list of authors, too!

No spam, no junk. That's a promise!

Sign Up Here

www.dragonbladepublishing.com

Dearest Reader;

Thank you for your support of a small press. At Dragonblade Publishing, we strive to bring you the highest quality Historical Romance from some of the best authors in the business. Without your support, there is no 'us', so we sincerely hope you adore these stories and find some new favorite authors along the way.

Happy Reading!

CEO, Dragonblade Publishing

Additional Dragonblade books by Author Elizabeth Keysian

Trysts and Treachery Series

Lord of Deception (Book 1)

Lord of Loyalty (Book 2)

Lord of the Forest (Book 3)

Lord of Mistrust (Book 4)

Lord of the Manor (Book 5)

Her Christmas White Knight (Novella)

The Grey Lady of The Manor (Novella)

The Lyon's Den Series

The Lyon and the Lamb

Other Lyon's Den Books

Into the Lyon's Den by Jade Lee
The Scandalous Lyon by Maggi Andersen
Fed to the Lyon by Mary Lancaster
The Lyon's Lady Love by Alexa Aston
The Lyon's Laird by Hildie McQueen
The Lyon Sleeps Tonight by Elizabeth Ellen Carter
A Lyon in Her Bed by Amanda Mariel
Fall of the Lyon by Chasity Bowlin
Lyon's Prey by Anna St. Claire
Loved by the Lyon by Collette Cameron
The Lyon's Den in Winter by Whitney Blake
Kiss of the Lyon by Meara Platt
Always the Lyon Tamer by Emily E K Murdoch
To Tame the Lyon by Sky Purington
How to Steal a Lyon's Fortune by Alanna Lucas
The Lyon's Surprise by Meara Platt
A Lyon's Pride by Emily Royal
Lyon Eyes by Lynne Connolly
Tamed by the Lyon by Chasity Bowlin
Lyon Hearted by Jade Lee
The Devilish Lyon by Charlotte Wren
Lyon in the Rough by Meara Platt
Lady Luck and the Lyon by Chasity Bowlin
Rescued by the Lyon by C.H. Admirand
Pretty Little Lyon by Katherine Bone
The Courage of a Lyon by Linda Rae Sande
Pride of Lyons by Jenna Jaxon
The Lyon's Share by Cerise DeLand
The Heart of a Lyon by Anna St. Claire

Into the Lyon of Fire by Abigail Bridges
Lyon of the Highlands by Emily Royal
The Lyon's Puzzle by Sandra Sookoo
Lyon at the Altar by Lily Harlem
Captivated by the Lyon by C.H. Admirand
The Lyon's Secret by Laura Trentham
The Talons of a Lyon by Jude Knight
To Claim a Lyon's Heart by Sherry Ewing

CHAPTER ONE

Lady Aylsham Foundlings' Hospital, London

"SO—THE TRUTH OF the matter, Mrs. Bellamy, is that you wish to purchase a child."

Lady Araminta Lamb flushed behind her mourning veil. She'd known this negotiation would prove difficult but hadn't anticipated the antagonism with which her generous offer was being met by Leo Chetwynd, Earl of Aylsham, Principal Trustee at the Lady Aylsham Foundlings' Hospital.

He speared her with his hard gaze, his uncompromising mouth offering no quarter. She knew a refusal was coming and she didn't know what to do. If this plan failed . . .

"Not at all." She managed to keep the quaver out of her voice. "I understand that any foundling would be happy to be taken into a good home. All I'm offering is a generous donation in the hopes that I may adopt such a one—preferably a newborn. I wouldn't call that *purchasing.*"

He steepled his fingers and gazed at her from the opposite side of the polished walnut desk. "In my book, that amounts to the same thing. You must surely know that the orphans here are *not* for sale. The yard in which they are currently playing is *not* a shop window. There would be a legion of legalities to consider even if you were considering a genuine adoption—impossible to adhere to when you refuse to give me any further information about yourself. Or had you intended the aforementioned sum as a bribe?"

Insufferable fellow! He didn't understand at all. How could she tell him who she really was when secrecy was essential to her plan? The Lamb family estates, her sister Belinda's health and her own future depended on her returning home with a child she could pass off as her own.

Was there no way to get around this stubborn nobleman? Perhaps she could talk to one of the other trustees of the institution—they might not carry their pride like some kind of trophy. *They* might actually recognize the business sense of the offer she was making.

"The matter is a delicate one, and I'm unable to offer you any further details. And I resent you impugning my character and suggesting my name's a false one."

He was half-right of course, damn him, since she was using her maiden name. But that didn't make her a bad person. *Did it?*

He stood, forcing her to stare up at him so she could meet his eyes. "Allow me to show you to the door."

"No. Wait! I'll increase the donation." It would make life difficult for herself and Belinda, but once she had control of the Lamb fortune, the amount would be of no consequence. Indeed—if Aylsham gave her what she needed and allowed her to meet the conditions of her late husband's will, she'd be able to make regular donations to the foundlings' charity.

Aylsham clasped his hands in front of him, drawing her eyes to the gold signet ring he wore on his little finger. He rotated this a couple of times, despite it being tight on his well-manicured hand, and cleared his throat.

"I apologize if you think me inconsiderate. I can tell by your apparel that you're recently widowed, and trust me—you have my deepest sympathies for your loss. But this plan of yours, whatever is behind it, is one you've not considered sensibly. I fully appreciate that grief can confuse both one's mind and one's heart. You should be thanking me for my refusal. Now, I'm certain you have other things that press upon your time. As do I."

He bowed and indicated the door.

What a pompous prig! It was as well her veil hid her expression. *She hoped.* Araminta rose from her seat, her mind working feverishly. She needed to produce a child before the year was out, and it mattered not who'd fathered it—Horatio's lawyer, who had more port in his veins than blood, hadn't been clear enough about that important fact, leaving her a loophole to exploit.

The only other way to secure her sister's future—and her own—would be to marry again. But after her grim four years of wedlock with Horatio Lamb, marriage was the very *last* thing she could contemplate.

If only things had been different! Belinda might have successfully delivered her illegitimate babe, and they could have returned from their secret exile with a child she could pretend was her own. Indeed, had she chosen to care for her husband rather than her sister, there might have been a faint chance of conceiving a legitimate heir. But only if she could have tolerated the touch of a bedridden, syphilitic man.

She shuddered. Intimacy with Horatio had always been torture—both physical and mental. Would it be the same with *any* man? Belinda had said not, but then Belinda had been besotted with her Lieutenant Coyle, who'd seduced her, then got himself killed on the Peninsula. Belinda had praised everything he did to the heavens. Oh, to be in love like that!

"Mrs. Bellamy?"

Dragging herself back to the here and now, Araminta ignored the tall man looming by the doorway and moved across to the window. Gazing out, she saw a bevy of small children playing in the courtyard. Poor Belinda! She still hadn't recovered from the loss of her child, even though Horatio had insisted it would have had to be given away. Belinda's thoughts were so melancholy, so muddled now. The last thing she needed was to lose her home because of the conditions of Horatio's will.

But an irresistible force stood in the way of Araminta's plan succeeding: Lord Aylsham.

She needed some thinking time. "Why do you have bars on these windows, my lord?" She touched them with trembling fingers.

Aylsham came to stand beside her. His closeness was oppressive, but she stood her ground.

"They are there for security reasons." He sounded irritated. "Because this is my office. I don't want you to imagine this place is a prison. The inmates get plenty of light and air."

He was evidently a man of little patience. She could perhaps try cajoling him, but there was no point fluttering her eyelashes or moistening her lips, as her face was hidden by a black lace veil. She couldn't lift it without running the risk of him recognizing her, even though she had no idea if they'd ever met before. Besides which, she'd vowed on Horatio's death to never again be cowed or commanded by a man.

She winced inwardly. Horatio's rule had been harsh and unrelenting. Her relief that he was gone was matched only by the dismay at discovering his will didn't protect his widow as it ought. Although perhaps she should have known that would be the case with *him*.

"That's as may be, sir, but the orphans can neither enter nor leave of their own volition, I take it?" Curse it—why had she said that aloud? She was merely provoking him further, risking the success of her mission.

Aylsham's breath hissed between his teeth. "I can assure you there's no similarity between this home and a prison. These children are cosseted, educated, and cared for. They'll be able to exercise their own judgment and make choices when they're old enough. They'll be free to enter the world beyond these walls as soon as we're certain they can find their way and will manage with little difficulty."

"You don't think the children would flourish even more in the bosom of a loving family?" For she would shower affection upon any child she could call her own. At one time, she'd been eager to give Horatio all her affection, but he'd mocked the idea of love within a marriage. Her love had been dammed up inside, rejected, eventually turning to poison and bitterness. Having a child in her life would turn her back into a human being again. It would certainly delight Belinda. But Lord Aylsham had no right to know any of that, the hateful fellow. Her pain must be kept hidden—it was the only way to survive.

The light from the window glittered like flint in his grey eyes as he faced her. "One could hardly call you, a widow, a 'loving family'. Were you to return here with a husband, your veil removed, and documentation to prove your identity, it would be an entirely different matter."

"Perhaps I should apply to the Board of Trustees—they might take a different approach." She knew she was grasping at straws now. Her inquiries had suggested that Aylsham's word was final on most matters to do with the charity. But there might be a loophole in the charity's constitution, just as there had been in Horatio's will.

Thank heaven for that mistake! Thank heaven also for the fact that she'd seen a copy of the will before returning home with Belinda to Forty Court. The wording required that a "child of his body *or* of his wife's, born within the first five years of their marriage" could inherit, with his wife administering the estates until that child came of age. The "or" should have been "and" but the Lamb family lawyer must have had one too many drinks when he'd checked the paper through.

Lord Aylsham sucked in a breath, reminding her of his presence. "I cannot prevent you from speaking to the other trustees, of course. It would be a waste of your time, however, as we have a charter and articles which would prevent any one person from doing something against the interests of the charity, the other trustees, or the children. How can I put it any more plainly? These children are *not* for sale."

It took all her willpower not to slap him, odious creature! But he was too broad-shouldered, too strongly erect and stiff. It would be like hitting a brick wall—which his nature very much resembled.

"Society will be interested to discover you don't have the children's best interests at heart."

His mouth twitched. "Blackmail, Mrs. Bellamy? Do you think I'm afraid of gossip?"

She glanced sideways at his raven-black hair, his determined chin, and unrelenting expression.

"Perhaps you *should* be," she retorted, then instantly regretted her words. She was losing this battle. She needed to retreat and regroup. Ducking her head, she maneuvered around him toward the door. "I'd better go."

He strode across the room and held the door open for her again. "Exactly what I've been telling you. Farewell, Mrs. Bellamy."

She tried to keep her head high and her shoulders straight as she walked down the corridor. A uniformed beadle bowed to her and opened the double doors onto the busy London street.

Behind her, she could still hear the laughter and shouts of the children at play, and her heart clenched painfully in her chest. Tears stung her eyes. The encounter with Lord Aylsham had bruised and shaken her, and she narrowly avoided being struck by a stylish barouche as it sped over the cobbles of Wren Street.

"Put yourself together, woman. You have to be the strong one."

She sucked in deep breaths of the chill spring air, and wryly noted the date—it was the Ides of March, an ominous date indeed. Perhaps she should not have expected a successful endeavor at such an inauspicious time.

The wind whipped at her skirts as she turned the corner into the street where her carriage had been left, out of sight of curious eyes. The carriage was draped in black, pronouncing her a widow but not revealing the Lamb family crest. It was essential that her business in London be conducted anonymously.

Her coachman alighted to hand her up into the carriage, where Belinda was waiting for her, her beautiful face pale and strained.

She stared at Araminta, at her hands, and then behind her. Her jaw dropped.

The carriage lurched into movement as Belinda exclaimed, "You haven't got one! You said you were going to get a baby!"

Araminta seized her sister's hand. It wouldn't do for the girl to have one of her tantrums in a carriage in the middle of the street. She still hadn't forgotten the awful moment Belinda had learned of the impossible terms of Horatio's will and had torn at her face and hair, howling like a banshee as the blood began to flow. She gave the hand in hers a reassuring squeeze.

"These things take time, my darling. And the wheels of the law move slowly, so we have just as much time as we need to make things right."

And she *would* make things right.

The last thing she wanted was for the unstable Belinda to be put into an asylum. She must give the girl whatever she needed to make her secure and happy. An adopted child would be a boon to them both, but if the intolerable Lord Aylsham could not be swayed, there were only two alternatives.

Both were drastic and riddled with risk. She must become pregnant immediately and return to Forty Court with a child before the year was out. Or she must find herself a husband at excessively short notice.

There was one thing she could do that might achieve *both* ends, but it would mean entering a place where no lady ought to go—she must pay a visit to the most notorious gambling house in London.

She must enter the Lyon's Den.

Chapter Two

"WE COULD DO with a lick of paint in here." The Honorable Roland Chetwynd, Leo's younger brother, glanced at the bare walls of the study. "Are we too poor now to keep up appearances in the London house?"

Leo frowned. "Don't remind me." He reached across his desk for the brandy decanter, poured himself a generous measure, then put some back. If he was to keep the Foundlings' Home free from interference, he needed to save every penny.

"We should hear about the return on my investment very soon. All our problems will be over then," Leo added.

Roland did a turn around the room, then came to a halt in front of the desk, staring pointedly at the decanter.

With a sigh, Leo poured another brandy and handed it to him. "You can't tell me one minute you're concerned that we're short of money, and the next, demand to drink my brandy."

The irrepressible Roland tossed his head back and laughed. "It is not so bad as all that, surely?"

Leo took a sip and swilled the liquor around his mouth, then swallowed, relishing its fiery transit down his throat. He was still completely out of sorts, as he had been since his encounter with that wretched widow at the Foundlings' Hospital. It was unlike him to be rude to a woman, but he knew he had been. Unforgivably so, considering she'd just lost her husband. However, the truth remained that her proposal had sounded very much like a purchase, and that was *not* what he had in mind for the children that he, and Mama before him, had nurtured so carefully.

"I shouldn't imagine paint is all that expensive. I could no doubt do the job myself if push came to shove."

"An admirable attitude." But Leo knew full well that Roland would make a mull of things. His charm, good looks, and an uncanny ability to lose at cards were what made him popular amongst the *ton*. He had no other skills whatsoever—he'd make an unreliable husband, a mutinous soldier, and a lazy curate. There seemed to be no place for Roland in the world but as a perpetual younger brother, supported by good will and the family money. Of which there was little available at present, world trade being what it was. If only the ships he'd invested in would return home with their cargo of cotton!

"Why don't you let the Foundlings' Hospital go? I'm sure Mama never expected you to put so much of the family money into it. The other trustees should put in more of the finances. Or you could set up a subscription scheme like I've seen mentioned in the papers. Your contribution would be your time since you're so excellent at organizing things. The Chetwynd family coffers would no longer be under strain while we're waiting for your cotton."

Leo rose from behind his desk, stalked across to the fireplace, and pushed at the fender with his boot. They'd had this conversation too many times for his liking.

"I know you mean well, Roland. But you have to trust me on this."

Roland pulled a face. "But how can I manage on the measly allowance you give me?"

"Don't push me. Just because you're my brother doesn't mean I can't throw you out on your ear. Regardless of the gossip that would cause."

Something he might very well do if Roland kept coming home in the evenings with empty pockets that had previously been full. Ah, well—at least the man didn't keep an expensive mistress or dangle after some opera singer who required valuable jewelry.

Roland joined him by the fire and clapped him on the back. "I love you too, brother. And I know exactly what you're thinking—that I shouldn't gamble. But I can't see the difference between you and me. Your business venture into cotton importing is a far greater gamble and a much higher risk than anything *I've* done."

Leo glanced away. His brother had a point, but Leo was too proud to admit it.

"Remember—it's not just luck that commands the card table," Roland continued. "There's skill too, a skill that builds with experience. One night I shall come home with several sets of vowels in my pocket—for property, a horse perhaps, jewelry, or even a fortune in coin."

Leo sighed. Normally, such a conversation would be little more than banter between the two brothers. Hurts, insults, or arguments would be easily brushed off with no harm done. But tonight, he was out of temper due to that encounter with Mrs. Bellamy.

Still, he made an effort. "Point taken," he managed. "Can we please change the subject now?" He warmed his brandy in front of the fire. The flickering lights reflecting from the carved crystal soothed him. "Have you ever heard of a Mrs. Bellamy?"

Roland grinned. "A new squeeze of yours? An abandoned wife? A lonely widow? It's high time you took up with the fair sex again. It would improve your temper no end."

"Nothing like that." The very idea! "She was thoroughly objectionable—the worst kind of woman. She wanted to buy a child."

"Really?" Roland leaned closer, interested. "Did she say why?"

"No." Leo hadn't thought to ask her. Why should her business or her reasons mean anything to him? No sooner had he heard her request than he'd wanted her out of his office.

"Her proposition was, quite frankly, insulting."

Roland tutted. "Have you no curiosity whatsoever, brother? What sort of woman was she? Hard-nosed and business-like? Foolish and naïve? Wicked and manipulative?"

Leo ran a finger around the rim of his glass, then placed it on the mantelpiece. He stroked the signet ring Elinora had given him. The so-called Mrs. Bellamy had been none of those things.

"I should say 'desperate' was more the word." As well as extremely stubborn.

"And are you now feeling guilty at having refused a damsel in distress?"

"Quite the opposite. She lied to me—I'm absolutely certain the name she gave was false. She was dressed in mourning but in the costliest fabric, and her speech and deportment were highly refined." In fact, she'd reeked of nobility. If only he could have seen beneath the veil . . .

"So—had you allowed her to make a donation and adopt a foundling, that child would, quite possibly, have enjoyed a life of luxury. You've now snatched that opportunity away. I understand—guilt makes you cross. It always has."

"I do *not* feel guilty!" Leo threw back another mouthful of brandy. "I was quite within my rights to refuse someone who wouldn't give me their true identity. One cannot trust a person who has something to hide. Let that be an end to it—I refuse to discuss it anymore."

Roland rolled his eyes, then glanced outside. "I think I should like to go out for a walk. Will you join me?"

"No. Forgive me. I'm weary from a full day at the home. I've been playing games with the children, which is more exhausting than you can possibly imagine." He stared at his brother. "You ought to come and spend some time with them—Mama would've wanted you to."

"Maybe. And perhaps, in the meantime, I can make some inquiries about this Mrs. Bellamy of yours, who seems to have got beneath your skin. In fact, I'll come and help you with the little orphans, if, in exchange, I can tempt you to one night at the tables."

Before Leo could react, his brother had raised his hand dismissively. "No, don't say me nay yet. We'll take a limited amount of money each—we'll just leave if we make no progress. But if one day soon, you come to the Lyon's Den with me, I can assure you of a damned good meal and doubtless some unusual entertainment before play begins. The proprietress, Mrs. Dove-Lyon, is most inventive in the methods she uses for keeping gentlemen entertained. I'll have a word next time I'm there, and make sure she'll enroll you as a member. She knows pretty much everything about everyone, so there shouldn't be any problem getting you accepted.

"No doubt because you love sharing tittle-tattle." What had Roland been saying about him? Leo sucked in a breath. His brother was wearing his "brilliant idea" expression—it was time to be diplomatic, or they would end up crossing swords again.

"You'd better head out for your walk now before it gets dark. I swear there was rain on the wind. I felt a few spots as I rode home."

"Don't try to distract me. I have an excellent plan bouncing around in my head—I just need to get it straight. And as I keep telling you, if you used a carriage, you wouldn't need to worry about the weather."

As always, the hair rose on the back of Leo's neck. He had hated carriages with a passion ever since he'd fallen out of one as a child. But that was a secret he intended to take to his grave. No one need know that the great, the benevolent, the well-connected, the *impeccable* Earl of Aylsham was frightened of carriages.

"I think I'll settle down with the newspaper." He took up a copy of *The Courant* and chose the chair closest to the fireplace, then pretended to be deeply absorbed, in hopes that his brother would not pursue his "idea" any further.

Roland drummed his fingers on the edge of the desk, blithely ignoring the hint. "I'll go in a moment. But I've just thought of something that will solve all our financial problems. One of us must marry an heiress! Preferably *you,* as you're the better catch."

Leo closed his eyes and thrust away the pain. He'd been married once and had lost both wife and child at the same time. The agony of Elinora's loss, and that of their baby son, had never diminished.

He lifted his hand and pressed his lips to the signet, saluting her memory. Keeping his voice as level as his shattered emotions would allow, he said, "I have no objection to *you* marrying an heiress, Roland. But please, leave me out of it. I refuse to put my neck in the noose of matrimony again. I remain true to the memory of Elinora and intend to spend the rest of my days as a bachelor. It's far simpler that way—I have enough responsibility with the estates, the Foundlings' Hospital, and my investments." It had been almost three years since he'd lost his wife, but it felt like yesterday. He never wanted to endure such agony of loss again.

"I don't think you understand the complexities of marriage, Roland," he continued. "Our parents made it appear simple, but I can assure you, it's not. You'd have to give up some of your ways if *you* were to wed, and I can't see you liking that at all."

"Oh, but it had far better be you, Leo. You have more to offer an heiress than I do. A title for a start, and good standing in society. Perhaps you should marry an American—I hear they adore titles. Then you can stop fretting over the hospital, we can get the townhouse painted, *and* do something about the roof at Brampton Hall."

"Heiresses don't grow on trees. I don't know how you plan on discovering such a one."

Dammit. He hadn't meant to sound interested. His brother would see it as encouragement.

"Begging your pardon, Leo, you've lived like a hermit since Elinora's demise. You know nothing of what goes on in London society, either the better half or the demimonde. Mrs. Dove-Lyon deals in heiresses." Roland jutted his chin forward, as he always did when he warmed to a subject. "Those in need of a husband employ her as a matchmaker. And from what I've heard, not a single couple she's united in matrimony has had anything to complain of. Her methods are somewhat unusual, but I can assure you that they're always successful. If you make it known that you're available, she'll find you a wealthy wife, sure as eggs is eggs."

Leo folded his paper and flung it down in exasperation. "Please curb your enthusiasm, brother. I have no intention whatsoever of falling in with your plans. From the sound of it, *you* shouldn't either—this Mrs. Dove-Lyon sounds like a denizen of the London underworld. Neither she nor her gambling den can be trusted."

Roland's response was cut off by a knock on the door.

"Come."

In reply to Leo's command, a footman entered, bearing a letter on a silver salver.

"A note for your lordship," he announced, bowing and backing away as soon as Leo picked up the missive.

He frowned. The handwriting was one he recognized and had learned to dread. "It's from that dreadful Pargeter," he growled, ripping open the letter.

"Pargeter?"

"You know, that rich-as-Croesus interloper who's after the land on which the Foundlings' Hospital stands. He's certain he can make a mint out of it and keeps increasing his offer. The other trustees aren't as conscientious as I am—one day, they'll cave. The orphans will be forced to move out to the country, where there are no prospects."

"Any new premises needn't be too far out of town, surely? There are stagecoaches and mail coaches aplenty to keep you connected with what London has to offer."

Leo grimaced. "The children will hate the upheaval." As would he. "The move could end up being extremely expensive. And if Pargeter reneges on the deal, we could find ourselves bankrupt halfway through the process and stuck in a lengthy court battle to get the rest of the money out of him. It's too risky."

He stared at the note and the temptingly increased offer written there, then screwed the paper into a tight little ball and cast it into the fire, staring angrily as the flames consumed it. He rather wished they were consuming the writer, too.

"Then perhaps you *should* consider my suggestion and see if there are any wealthy widows in search of a decent, upright husband such as yourself. Come with me to the Lyon's Den and at least see what the place has to offer. I can assure you that you'll enjoy your evening, even if you don't come away with a fortune in your pocket or a fiancée on your arm."

"You're incorrigible." Leo stared gloomily into the flames. Maybe Roland was right. Would it be betraying Elinora's memory if he were to step out into the light of society again—and perhaps even do something foolish but fun?

Roland tugged at his sleeve and made puppy eyes at him.

Leo couldn't help but smile. "Very well. I shall consider dining at the Lyon's Den. I'm not going to get myself involved in anything more complicated than that, however."

Unless he received word that the merchant ships had run into difficulties on the voyage. If that happened, he might find himself grateful for whatever scheme his brother, or the mysterious Mrs. Dove-Lyon, could come up with for him.

CHAPTER THREE

IT HAD TAKEN Araminta over a week to build up the courage but now here she was, standing in front of the blue-painted building on Cleveland Row known as the Lyon's Den. The carriage was tucked down a back street several blocks away, and she was once again incognito behind her mourning veil.

Drawing in a breath, she took a step forward, but before she could touch the knocker, a shape materialized in front of her, barring her way. She repressed a scream, and looked up, then looked up still more until she met the eyes of the giant now obstructing her. He wore a dour expression and carried one gloved hand stiffly against his side—a war wound, no doubt. He had the harsh, haunted look of a veteran. It was as much as she could do not to take a step back, or even turn tail.

But she was Lady Araminta Lamb, Respectable Widow, and had decided not to be cowed by anybody, particularly men. Her business might not be in the least bit respectable, but nobody needed to know that. *Yet.*

"Good morning, madam. I must inform you that the ladies' entrance is around the side."

"Oh. But I have business with the proprietress, Mrs. Dove-Lyon."

Surely, she didn't look like a servant or a tradesperson? She lifted her chin and glared at the man.

He sketched her a bow. "I beg your pardon, but this entrance is for gentlemen only. I shall conduct you to the ladies' entrance and make sure Mrs. Dove-Lyon knows you're here. What name shall I give?"

Should she call herself Mrs. Bellamy again? Would that not get her into all kinds of hot water with Mrs. Dove-Lyon? Although she'd heard rumors about the Lyon's Den, it had been impossible to substantiate any of them or to be absolutely certain of the names of those involved in the scandals that emanated from that place. Evidently, the proprietress knew how to be discreet.

"Can I rely on your discretion, Mr. er—"

"They call me Titan, ma'am."

Of course, they did. Although Atlas or Hercules would probably have done just as well. Despite his appearance, the man knew his manners.

She lowered her voice. "Please inform Mrs. Dove-Lyon that Lady Araminta Lamb is here."

The giant nodded again, then ushered her around the side of the building to an alternative entrance. Opening the door, he invited Araminta to precede him up some steps, through a robing room, and into a well-appointed parlor.

"If you would care to be seated, Lady Lamb, I'll send word to Mrs. Dove-Lyon. Can I offer you refreshment?"

She tried to picture this larger-than-life creature pouring tea into a delicate porcelain cup and failed. Anyway, her stomach was tied in such a knot, it would reject anything she tried to put into it.

She shook her head. "No, thank you."

The man vanished just as suddenly as he'd appeared, and she was left to gaze around the room. But her brain took in nothing of her surroundings. She was seething with nerves, and it took every ounce of her strength not to retreat from this strange place where a woman ruled the roost, where men lost fortunes and gained wives by devious means, and wagers were laid on the most imaginative of outcomes. There was supposedly a floor upstairs where unmentionable happenings occurred. Certainly not a safe place for a vulnerable young widow to be.

Araminta squared her shoulders. She'd stood her ground with the intractable Earl of Aylsham, hadn't she? And here, she was a bona fide customer with enough money—she hoped—to afford Mrs. Dove-Lyon's extortionate fees, so she shouldn't feel threatened. She must think of Belinda—she was doing this for her sister as much as for herself. Belinda called Forty Court home and needed to be restored to that place of security before she slipped any further into melancholia.

A door opened, and with a rustle of bombazine, a veiled woman, attired all in black, entered the room and offered her hand to Araminta.

"Lady Lamb. Please accept my condolences on the recent loss of your husband."

"Allow me to return the same sentiment to yourself."

Mrs. Dove-Lyon laughed as she indicated a chair and took another for herself. "Be seated. And please—I don't need your sympathy. My husband is long gone. I have my reasons for choosing to continue in this garb. However, I would be most gratified if you could remove your veil, as I'd like to see with whom I'm dealing. I assume you're here as a client?"

Araminta lifted her veil and hoped that her skin was not too pale and her thick, chestnut hair not too untidy. She wanted to make a good impression on the mysterious woman in front of her.

"You refused Titan, but perhaps *I* may offer you something?"

"No, thank you." Araminta wanted her visit to be as brief as possible, while her courage still held.

"Very well." Mrs. Dove-Lyon folded her hands in her lap and tilted her head to one side. "Tell me what I can do for you."

"I assume that what I say to you will go no further?" If only she could see the woman's face! It was impossible to assess someone's trustworthiness when their expression was hidden.

"Discretion is our watchword. There's no need to tell me any more than is necessary, of course. I don't wish you to feel uncomfortable."

"I have urgent need of a child. If I don't deliver an heir to the Lamb estates in the next twelve months, they'll pass to my husband's cousin, Thomas Bilson. I know—you're asking yourself how I can produce an heir when my husband's dead, but the circumstances are peculiar. The lawyer's wording requires an heir of Lord Lamb's body *or* of mine. It ought to have said, 'of his body *and* mine,' but it doesn't. So, if I conceive a child of my own, the estate will pass to me in trust and to them when they come of age."

Mrs. Dove-Lyon sniffed and raised her head. "I do not deal in male prostitution here, Lady Lamb. This is not some kind of human stud farm, whatever you may have heard."

Araminta flushed. "I wasn't thinking of that." She hadn't been, had she? "I've come to put the facts before you and be guided by you. I understand you're in a position to help women who find themselves in . . . difficulty. I don't seek your assistance only for myself. My sister, who is but seventeen, has reaped the rewards of a foolish infatuation. The resulting child was born too early and was lost, and even though we've thus far avoided a scandal, she's not been herself since. To keep her out of the asylum, I'll do *anything*. But I cannot secure her future without an heir—it's the only way to keep a roof over both Belinda's head and mine."

"There are well-established methods for adopting children. But I don't know how your plan could work. You could adopt a child and pretend it was your own, but with a young baby, there's no way of knowing what it will look like when grown. If you were unlucky, it would look not the least bit like yourself. Your ploy would soon be exposed."

"I know." She'd chewed over that problem during many a sleepless night. "In any case, I met an obstacle on my very first attempt to adopt a child."

Mrs. Dove-Lyon lifted her head. "Do you have no finances at your disposal? Did your husband give you no allowance? I'm sure you needn't have given up at the first hurdle."

Araminta hung her head. "The problem was not a financial one—I have enough funds at present." *Just.* "I was not allowed to adopt because I wouldn't reveal my true identity. That is unacceptable, it seems."

"Hmm. You mean that you could not reveal yourself as Lady Lamb because your family is too well-known. It would be too late to pretend any child is your husband's. Were you thinking of vanishing for a while and returning with a young baby?"

Araminta nodded. She *could* go away again, and pretend on her return to have had an affair that resulted in the birth of a child. But there would be questions asked and investigations made, especially since she'd produced no heir during Horatio's lifetime.

As if reading her thoughts, Mrs. Dove-Lyon continued, "The general consensus in your husband's family is doubtless that you're barren. You could still lose everything, including your reputation, if you try, and fail, to hoodwink them. I dread to think what might happen to your sister then."

Put that way, Araminta's scheme sounded desperate indeed. She'd come to Mrs. Dove-Lyon for help, but all the woman was doing was pouring cold water on everything. She rose.

"I'm wasting my time here."

"No." Mrs. Dove-Lyon gestured her back to her seat. "I'm not easily defeated, as you will discover. I have an alternative suggestion to your adoption plan—something that will stand up to scrutiny."

Araminta's heart sped up. There was still hope? She sat.

"I broker marriages here at the Lyon's Den. It is clear to me that *that* would be the best solution for you."

"Oh, no—"

"Pray, hear me out. I'm renowned for making matches that last. If I find you a suitable husband, you can expect him to be all you could wish for. If he fails to get you with child within the first couple of months of your union, you can still carry out your subterfuge. You can appear to be increasing, invent a health issue that requires you to go away somewhere quiet, then return with a newborn that you've secretly adopted. Everyone will then assume that, whereas your first husband was impotent, your second husband is not. And if that ruse should fail, you will *still* have a husband to protect both you and your sister. How does that sound?"

It made sense, but it would be the last resort. The idea of spending a single day more under the suffocating control of a husband was anathema. Araminta had barely begun to make use of her newfound freedom, and now that she'd tasted it, she had no intention of giving it up.

But maybe she should go along with Mrs. Dove-Lyon's plan for the time being since it was all she had. It would, at least, give her some thinking time, and she needn't go through with the marriage if she found a better solution. Would she still be forced to hand over Mrs. Dove-Lyon's reputedly eye-watering fee if she changed her mind?

The French gilt clock over the mantelpiece seemed to tick more loudly, and the coal burning in the hearth sputtered and flared. The room was closing in on her and she wished that she could hide behind *her* veil so that Mrs. Dove-Lyon would not see how very desperate she was, how very much she needed this.

"I . . . I'm not sure it's what I want."

"I will find you the perfect husband, Lady Lamb. That is my forte. But he'll want something in return. Can you keep a husband who may have no more than a modest income? When your heir comes of age and receives full powers over the estate, will he—or she—provide for the pair of you and your sister?"

She sincerely hoped so, but *that* outcome was out of her hands. "We can live comfortably enough while I administer the estate. The trust will provide an annual allowance to cover running costs and the upkeep of the townhouse, plus expenses. My new husband won't be marrying into a fortune, but he'll be able to enjoy its proceeds."

She bit her lip. There was one further stipulation in the will, one which she hadn't disclosed to anyone. It meant she could not control or influence the heir or be absolutely certain that said heir would provide for her in her dotage. Horatio had decreed that the child would be snatched from her before she'd had time to build a bond with it and fostered out. Araminta was not to be given the opportunity to love and nurture her own child.

What husband, what father would agree to such terms? She'd despise anyone who did—*not* a good basis for wedlock.

She could feel Mrs. Dove-Lyon's eyes boring into her from behind her veil, and prayed it wasn't obvious that she was hiding something.

After a moment, the woman nodded. "Very well. You can leave this matter in my hands—I already have some candidates in mind. I'll send you my fee in due course—I won't have an exact figure until I've finalized the details. I must advise you, Lady Lamb, that you may have to sacrifice a great deal to achieve your ends, and I don't just mean money. Once you've accepted my terms, you'll be bound by them. I'll have a legal contract written up." She waved one hand dismissively. "Don't worry—I'll be discreet. No one need know of our arrangement unless you decide to renege."

Araminta sucked in a breath. Mrs. Dove-Lyon was going to help her! But could she trust the woman? Horatio had crushed her spirit, making it almost impossible to trust *anyone.*

But the word was that the Lyon's Den delivered what it promised—if that were untrue, the establishment would never have prospered, and nor would its owner.

She'd have to tread a careful path to ensure she got what she needed. She also had to hope no one found out about that clause concerning fostering in case it proved an insurmountable obstacle.

Sending up a silent prayer, Araminta held out her hand to shake on the deal. "I can't thank you enough." Reaching into her reticule, she handed over a card. "Here is my direction. Please send your bill and your contract via sealed letter to this address, and I'll respond immediately."

Mrs. Dove-Lyon's voice was warm as she said, "I promise to find you a husband to both love and cherish, far more than you might have imagined possible. I predict not only good fortune, but much pleasure in your future, only . . . you must agree to whatever scheme I devise for you, even if it goes against your better nature. I trust you understand that the end justifies the means."

Araminta *did* understand, and it sent a flurry of butterflies whirling around in her stomach. Love? Pleasure? *Could* such things be had with a man? She doubted it.

Mrs. Dove-Lyon bade her farewell and, in response to her call, Titan reappeared and escorted Araminta from the premises. She flipped her veil down before anyone could see her, pulled her cloak tightly around her shoulders, and set her face against the chill March wind that eddied between the buildings of Cleveland Row.

Belinda was waiting in the carriage. It was never wise to leave Belinda alone at the best of times, but knowing the importance of this particular visit, she couldn't be persuaded to remain at their lodgings where she would at least have had servants about her. Araminta must decide what to share with her sister and what to keep to herself—it wouldn't do to excite the girl.

She flushed, thinking back over her conversation with Mrs. Dove-Lyon. The woman had mentioned pleasure. There was no doubt she'd meant the marriage bed—a place where Araminta had found no joy whatsoever. And yet, she must endure it again if she was to conceive a child.

By the time she reached the carriage, the cold air had cleared her head, and the flush had subsided. Was she doing the right thing? Or was she about to rush headlong into the most terrible mistake of her life?

She had to risk it. She simply *had* to. Because if this ploy failed, both she and Belinda would end up destitute.

CHAPTER FOUR

AFTER A FURTHER two weeks of agonizing soul-searching and uncertainty, Araminta was forced to act. The early shoots of April already bedecked the plane trees bracketing the London streets and she knew she was running out of time.

Her decision having been made, she was now ensconced in the ladies' private room at the Lyon's Den, awaiting the details of her fate from Mrs. Dove-Lyon.

A woman Araminta had never seen before swept into the room and introduced herself as Hermia. She curtsied, announcing, "I've come to prepare you for the night's entertainment, ma'am. Allow me to assist you with the removal of your clothes."

Araminta glanced around the room. It held various masquerade costumes on mannequins—the perfect way for her to maintain anonymity throughout the proceedings.

Putting aside her gloves, reticule, veiled bonnet, and winter pelisse, she waited patiently as she was divested of her remaining clothing. Worryingly, Hermia didn't stop at her underclothes but insisted on continuing until she was naked and barefoot. A black cloak was thrown around Araminta's shoulders, presumably for warmth while her costume was readied. It was thus a great shock when Hermia gave a brief nod of farewell and left the room.

As Araminta stood in the middle of the floor battling the urge to dress and run for dear life, the door opened again. She spun to face it, clutching the cloak tightly around her neck, acutely aware of her state of undress beneath it.

It was Mrs. Dove-Lyon, accoutered in her customary black, but wearing a dark cloak that matched Araminta's and a full-face classical mask of comedy. She bore a tray.

"Good evening, Lady Lamb." The widow's tone was warm. "You must think my methods peculiar, but I assure you, you'll have the result you want by the end of the night. You should be warm enough in your cloak—I've ordered the staff to keep the fires well stoked. Here's something to fortify you while we wait."

The Lyon's Den proprietress sounded gleeful—she must be in her element when there was a matchmaking scheme in progress. Cowering within her cloak, Araminta hoped she could share the lady's optimism.

"A simple repast of bread and fruit. And wine, of course. But I've added spices—as you're going to meet your future husband tonight, your breath should smell sweet."

Araminta's stomach rose in revolt at the idea of food, but she took the glass gratefully and sipped. The liquid tasted delicious, and it had been mulled—she was tempted to quaff it in the most unladylike fashion but was aware of Mrs. Dove-Lyon's intense regard through the eyeholes of her mask.

"Thank you." She cleared her throat. "Which masquerade costume will I be wearing?"

Mrs. Dove-Lyon crossed the room to a mannequin draped in a Grecian-style gown and removed the mask of tragedy suspended from it. She held it out.

Araminta stared at it. "Is this *all?*"

"Indeed. There's to be a lottery tonight, and you're the first prize. Whoever wins will spend the night with you, after which you'll be married at the earliest opportunity. Gentlemen tend not to refuse to wed one of my clients after they've bedded them."

Araminta almost dropped her glass. She took a fortifying swig of the wine. "What exactly do you mean by *bedded* them?"

"There's an upstairs room prepared for you and the successful candidate. You're a widow, Lady Lamb, not a blushing virgin, and no stranger to the marriage bed. You will, therefore, have discovered by now how important it is that your husband should not only be agreeable to you by day but acceptable to you by night. If the gentleman you choose from the three I've found for you isn't to your taste, then the plan will be repeated with my second or third choice. Don't look so alarmed! I don't mean for them to bed you one after the other—there would be a proper time interval between. However, I'm renowned for my ability to choose well and I believe you'll enjoy tonight more than you have enjoyed any other night since you were first wed."

Araminta collapsed into a chair. It was now abundantly plain that she was *not* to spend the latter part of the evening in polite conversation over tea and muffins with her prospective suitors. She was shocked, outraged, fascinated—overwhelmed by such a jumble of emotions that she couldn't speak. Obviously, she must refuse to go along with this abominable plan. It was something that polite society would abhor—she would no longer be a respectable widow, but a scandalous one, eschewed by the *ton*.

Eventually, she found her voice. "You mean that the gentleman is to make intimate love to me?"

"Yes. For your sake *and* his. He is truly a gentleman and will offer you marriage as soon as I make your identity known to him. That, I can guarantee."

There it was again, the word *marriage*. Araminta repressed a shudder, then took another deep draft of her wine as her mind started heading off in a truly wicked direction.

What if she should become pregnant by tonight's encounter? She would then bear a child of her own body within the year and adhere to the conditions of Horatio's will. It would solve all her problems—save the one of giving the child to foster parents almost immediately. But there might be time to think of a way around that, might there not? And she need not marry at all!

However, the agreement with Mrs. Dove-Lyon had been written up as a proper contract, signed, and sealed. It was what she'd paid out a massive two hundred sixty guineas for. When she told the woman that she no longer wanted to marry the man who'd bedded her, would she be able to claw the money back? Taking a stand against Mrs. Dove-Lyon risked exposure and an appalling scandal.

She must appear to go along with the plan for the moment. She must also drink much more wine—gallons of the stuff if possible—and overcome her aversion to male sexual advances.

"Must I truly remain naked under here?"

Mrs. Dove-Lyon chuckled behind her mask. "It's as necessary as the wine. I want you to be in a relaxed mood when your gentleman comes to claim you. It would ruin the moment entirely if you caviled, giggled like an idiot, proved to be ticklish, or ran away the moment he started to undress you. We need to show him that we mean business. By bedtime, you'll be used to your current state, I assure you. You might even begin to enjoy it."

"Have you tried this ploy before?"

"I won't give away my secrets. In any case, I always suit the arrangements to the client."

Somewhere a clock chimed the hour, and a burst of male laughter could be heard from the depths of the house.

"The men have almost finished their dinner. Will you view them before the tables are cleared for the entertainment?"

For a moment, Araminta experienced an unusual sense of power. For the first time in her life, she would get to *choose.* Heaven help her if she made the wrong decision! Maybe she needed a clear head after all. She set her glass down, seized some bread and an apple, and consumed them quickly.

Mrs. Dove-Lyon indicated the door. "Follow me."

It felt sinful padding along the corridors in her bare feet, her body swathed in the cloak and her face hidden behind the mask—she'd never felt so exposed. Her stomach fizzed with excitement at the knowledge that nobody knew what the cloak concealed. It was wickedly delicious and deliciously wicked, and she hoped she wouldn't burn in hell for it.

Mrs. Dove-Lyon led her to a balcony looking down onto an open area. The room was set out for dining, and the noise hit Araminta as soon as she stepped out onto the balcony.

Men were talking, laughing, clapping one another upon the back, rattling knives and plates, and drinking toasts. They were swathed in dark cloaks identical to her own, although she caught glimpses of evening clothes underneath.

Their masks were only half-face, but since they were dining, the only distinguishing feature she could see was the color of their hair. So, how on earth was she to choose from the twenty or so gentlemen below?

It was then that she noticed a few of them had gold trim around their hoods. "The ones with the gold on their hoods—why are there only three?"

"They are the men who'll win the three lottery grand prizes. As I've already mentioned, a night with you is the first prize."

"And the second, and the third?" Araminta peered down at the three men. Were there any clues to their ages, or their physical appearance?

"The second prize is a bolt of Chinese silk that I purchased from a warehouse yesterday. And the third is a Jeroboam of Champagne. I don't waste my clients' money on anything not worth winning."

One of the chosen gentlemen appeared to have very dark hair, but in the glittering candlelight, it was difficult to tell. The others were either mousy or blond, at a guess. If only she could see their faces!

"How did you choose these three?"

"Again, I won't reveal my methods, but they involve considerable research. I assure you—no one will be harmed when you choose your future spouse. There are no mistresses, no one to whom the men are already engaged, and no young females with expectations concerning them. The gentlemen are, in their own words, confirmed bachelors, but all will be well aware of the risks—and the rewards—of becoming involved in one of my gambling evenings."

"I'm glad to hear it." She'd hate to ruin another woman's hopes.

A wave of dizziness suddenly swept over her, and she reached for the chair that had been set out. Foolish woman! Why hadn't she taken more of the food when it was offered? She rested her chin on the balustrade and continued staring at the gentlemen so blissfully unaware of her existence.

Time became a blur. She forgot Mrs. Dove-Lyon—her senses were entirely focused on the three men with the gilt-edged hoods. One of them, she decided, was blond, because every time he moved into the bright center of the hall, his hair glittered like dark gold.

But her eyes kept returning to the dark-haired gentleman, following him as everyone milled around, choosing one of the entertainments set up in each corner of the room. He hovered uncertainly in the middle, and she sensed his tension—he didn't know which table to go to and appeared uncertain of his place amongst this company. A misfit in society, perhaps? Just like herself, then.

Another masked gentleman, rather shorter of stature, grasped the dark-haired man's arm and escorted him to one of the tables. She enjoyed the way Mr. Raven-hair moved, with an animal grace that reminded her of a proud stag in the forest.

Stop staring at him. There are two others that you're meant to be considering.

She scanned the room. The blond gentleman had joined a table that had several glasses, a pitcher, and a large empty basin beside it on the floor.

"What are they doing at those tables there?"

Mrs. Dove-Lyon snorted. "Some of the foolish things with which gentlemen amuse themselves. The empty table is one where they'll be testing their strength against one another. It's not too serious and usually ends in laughter. The table with the drink is another way for men to test their mettle—the jug contains an emetic. They wager on who can retain the contents of their stomach the longest."

Araminta pulled a face. "And the other two tables?"

"One is for a cigar-smoking competition. As you can see, there's a large bowl on the floor next to the table, a pitcher of fresh water, and a homemade garlic and honey electuary for when they can't stop coughing."

What a ridiculous way to spend an evening! Were any of these men adults at all? Why had they not left these foolish competitions in the schoolroom where they belonged? Araminta began to doubt she would find a husband here with whom she could bear to spend a single minute.

"The gentlemen lay wagers on the outcome of all these contests. The final table offers the game of Hazard, where fortunes can be won or lost on the roll of the dice." Mrs. Dove-Lyon paused and glanced down. "You can learn a lot about a man by the entertainment he chooses."

Despite her fuddled state, Araminta understood. This was all part of the show that had been put on for her benefit, the one that would lead to her choosing the man who would bed her tonight and father her child.

She had no wish to spend an evening rumpling the sheets with a man who had cast up his accounts or who smelled like an over-smoked ham. Where had Mr. Raven-hair chosen to go?

Go to the Hazard table. Go to the Hazard table!

The blond was testing his stomach. The gentleman with mousy hair had opted for the Hazard table, a definite point in his favor. Mr. Raven-hair was being ushered toward that table too, but at the last moment, he pulled away and strode back to the arm-wrestling challenge.

Disappointment tugged at her—she *had* hoped he'd do something more intellectually challenging. All the same, she found herself compelled to watch, especially as the games on that table seemed to result in such hilarity.

It turned out that cheating was perfectly acceptable, and the friends of each pair of combatants did whatever they could to distract their opponents. There was hair-pulling, mask-plucking, the filling of hoods with unpleasant substances, and the removal of chairs just as the combatants sat down to test their strength against one another.

Araminta found herself smiling, though she shouldn't approve of such childish behavior. Raven-hair won his game. Of course, he did. With broad shoulders like that and a deep chest, he would surely win any game of strength against his peers. It was a struggle to tear her eyes away from him and see how her other potential suitors were getting on.

Blondie was casting up his accounts into the basin. Mousy-hair had moved on to the cigar-smoking and appeared to have set fire to his mask. Araminta rolled her eyes. If Mr. Raven-hair didn't come up to scratch, this was going to be a complete waste of time.

The sudden boom of a gong made her jump and stare around in alarm. Mrs. Dove-Lyon gestured that she should remain seated.

"This is the highlight of the evening," she said in a low voice. "Meet Petruschka."

A new person had joined them on the balcony. She was attired in sparkling gold, but very scantily so. The full length of her silk-clad legs was exposed, her arms also—and the cut of the costume she wore was dangerously low. There were gilded ostrich feathers in her curled coiffure, and she held a bag in one hand. The costume was so elaborate, it reminded Araminta of a painting's gilded frame.

The new arrival gave her a cursory glance. She wore no mask, but her expression was one of deep concentration. She reached for a short pole resting just inside the balustrade, and as it moved, Araminta realized it was attached to the ceiling by two ropes.

She let out a gasp as Petrushka climbed over the balustrade and launched herself into the air before swinging back and forth over the heads of the gentlemen. Everyone looked up, and her performance was met with gasps and applause.

Just the sight of her doing so dangerous a thing made Araminta giddy. But she felt even giddier when Mrs. Dove-Lyon announced, "It is now that you must make your choice. Petrushka has three gold tickets, each of which represents a prize for the gentlemen I've picked for you. Only one of these will be given to the man of your choice. The other gentlemen will get lottery tickets too, so they don't feel left out, but that is of no importance to you. Lady Lamb—you have but a few moments more in which to make up your mind so Petrushka can deliver the correct ticket to the man of your choice."

While Araminta was struggling to comprehend the decision she now had to make, Petrushka continued to fly over the heads of the gentlemen below, balancing on the swinging bar and taking up poses, some of which were decidedly provocative. Then, secure in the knowledge that she had everyone's attention, she swung in a great arc around the room, opened her bag with her teeth, and scattered the contents over everyone's heads.

Some of the men gave excited whoops and hastened to grab the tickets. Araminta desperately tried to find the dark head and gilded hood of the man who had caught her attention, but he wasn't joining in the flurry of grabbing hands. Too proud to do so, perhaps? Would he make a suitable husband for her if *that* was the kind of man he was? Then again, maybe she needed someone who was out of the common sort. All the other gentlemen in the room would have understood Horatio and his behavior. Only a man who stood out from the crowd tonight offered the chance of a different experience in marriage.

Mr. Raven-hair was still watching Petrushka's performance, while the rest were mostly engaged in reading and swapping their lottery tickets.

"Well? Have you chosen? I'll need to have Petrushka pulled back and informed before she tires."

Mrs. Dove-Lyon spoke as if she presided over such matters every day. She could have no idea how Araminta was feeling—a fish out of water, a woman placed in a position in which she had never expected to find herself. *A woman with more power than she was used to.* The choice Araminta made would not only affect the future of herself and Belinda but that of her child *and* of the man who had come to the Lyon's Den in search of a wife.

"I'm drawn to the tall, dark-haired gentleman." Her voice came out in an embarrassing squeak.

Mrs. Dove-Lyon had one of her men pull Petrushka back to the balcony, then nodded to Araminta. "It's the choice I hoped you'd make." There was a definite smile in her tone. "You'll find that you've spent your money wisely. I only ask that you use your time tonight equally wisely. Be the best that you can in his arms, but don't reveal your identity. I'll ask him not to speak, and I beg you to do the same. Your bodies will do the speaking for you, and then tomorrow, when you're both sober, the true negotiations will begin. I swear on my dead husband's grave, you won't regret your decision, and nor will your lover."

Araminta quivered at the sound of the word *lover* and remembered that she was naked beneath her cloak. It *did* feel rather sensuous—and fabulously sinful. Unlikely as it was, perhaps she might even enjoy the attentions of a man in whose best interest it was to impress her.

Mrs. Dove-Lyon whispered something to Petrushka. The performer nodded, then launched herself out on her swing again, and this time, she swung past the three gentlemen with the gilded hoods. She let out a loud *huzzah* as she approached each of them, causing them to duck in alarm. On the return swing, she reached into her bosom, took out some tickets, and handed them down to each man.

The dark-haired gentleman hesitated and didn't collect his ticket until the third swing. At that, Petrushka let out a piercing ululation that gained everyone's startled attention. Waving at them cheekily, she returned to the balcony, secured her swing, and disappeared into the depths of the house.

Down below, Mrs. Dove-Lyon's staff had returned, each bearing baskets which they took round so that the men could collect the prizes. The blond gentleman seemed very happy with his bolt of silk, and the mousy-haired one was thrilled with his Jeroboam of Champagne and performed a brief and rickety jig.

Mr. Raven-hair stared at his ticket for many moments, then shook his head as if unable to believe what he read there. He then began pacing around the room, and finally, he glanced up at the balcony and locked gazes with Araminta.

He knew. He knew he was looking at his prize. Her heart flipped in her breast and a shiver coursed through her.

He couldn't possibly know what—or rather, whom—he had won. She was far too well concealed for that. What mattered more was who *he* was since he was going to play such an important part in her life. Why could she not know his name, his status, or his occupation until after they'd spent the night together? It seemed cruel and strange, unfair to both of them that they should not know until much later what they had gained. *Or lost.*

She didn't move. Holding his gaze boldly, she wondered what

color his eyes were, and whether or not his features would be pleasant. No—what did that matter? It was what lay in his heart and mind that would determine what their future should be.

He remained staring at her silently for a moment longer, then gave her an elegant bow before turning to one of the many veterans who served Mrs. Dove-Lyon. He must have asked a question, because the fellow nodded his head, and the dark-haired man disappeared from view.

Araminta reached for her wineglass and was delighted to see it had been refilled. She drained it to the very last drop, then turned away from the balcony and saw the same female servant who'd undressed her, waiting for her.

She swallowed hard. This was it. Her future, and those whose futures depended upon her, rested on the encounter that was to come. By heaven, this plan *had* to work! Otherwise, she would be completely, utterly ruined.

CHAPTER FIVE

LEO FOLLOWED THE masked woman up the stairs. The night had taken on a dreamlike quality—in fact, if he hadn't made every effort to be moderate in his drinking, he might imagine he was drunk. Not that he was swaying or feeling as if he were about to cast up his accounts—it felt more as if there was a buffer between him and reality, and that nothing he did in this strange half-world truly mattered.

Only—it *did*. Somewhere above, so his lottery ticket had informed him, a woman who was in search of a husband awaited him. And he, as Roland had pointed out more times than he could remember, needed her inheritance.

No! This was wrong. Where was Roland? He was familiar with the Lyon's Den—why hadn't he put a stop to this tomfoolery?

Leo spun around, grabbed the handrail, and attempted to return to the dining room—only to discover his path blocked by two powerfully-built gentlemen, clad in the garb of servants. They bowed their heads politely, turned him back the way he'd been facing, and escorted him back up the stairs. Even in his befuddled state, he knew it wasn't wise to struggle with two giants on the stairs.

On the landing above, the female servant vanished, to be replaced by a woman dressed entirely in black and masked. Not the same woman he'd seen on the balcony before—his body didn't react at all to *this* one.

"Lord Aylsham, you're most welcome. Congratulations on winning tonight's grand prize. Trust me—you won't regret participating."

This must be the fabled Mrs. Dove-Lyon. He bowed. "I regret it already, ma'am. Is it permissible to refuse the prize?"

"It is, but I wouldn't advise it." Her tone was no longer friendly. "Particularly not in your case. You're concerned about the future of your foundlings' hospital. A certain Mr. Pargeter is keen on buying and demolishing the buildings so he can make commercial use of the land. You don't currently have the funds to prevent this. No, don't shake your head at me. You winning the grand prize was no coincidence."

Indeed—he suspected as much. Mrs. Dove-Lyon must have made inquiries about him. Had she been in league with that scoundrel, Roland? He'd have something to say about *that.*

She tapped his elbow with her fan. "Not only will you obtain a highly desirable young wife who can bring you a regular income, but you'll have made an ally of myself. I have many connections and can do you as much harm as I can do you good. So, you see, it's most certainly in your best interests to accept your prize."

It was a trap, as Leo had suspected when he'd been handed that ticket—he'd been deliberately targeted, so Roland *must* be in on the scheme. He didn't like having his hand forced by others, particularly when not in full control of his faculties. He'd been drugged—he must have been. It was the only explanation for his current state.

However, the opportunity of acquiring a wealthy wife *did* sound like a good prospect, although he preferred to judge for himself whether or not a woman was desirable. He'd be taking a less risky gamble than he had with the missing cotton shipments.

Besides—he wasn't only doing this for himself. He was doing it for the orphans, sacrificing himself for the good of the many. It was his own folly that had put the Foundlings' Hospital in jeopardy, and he ought to pay the price.

"Very well. Where is she? And *who* is she, more to the point?"

The hostess tilted her head to one side. "There'll be no introductions. There'll be no speech at all, in fact. You are to spend the night together. In the morning, so long as the lady is still agreeable to the arrangement, you may procure a special license—my contacts will smooth that process for you."

So, his would-be bride could refuse him, but he could not refuse *her*? That rankled. But it also filled him with a powerful determination to ensure the woman would *not* refuse him. He would make her want him—his pride could not permit any other outcome.

He pushed his shoulders back. "Then I'm ready. Take me to her, if you will."

Mrs. Dove-Lyon nodded. "When you step through the door, you'll find yourself in complete darkness. Don't be alarmed—there's very little in the room that you could trip over. Beside the door—you should be able to feel it when you walk in—is a chair. Disrobe and lay your clothes up on that chair."

Heat flowed into his cheeks. How could he be talking to a complete stranger, and a woman to boot, about something so intimate as undressing? The situation was too peculiar—maybe he was asleep and having a bizarre dream. Had he eaten something at supper that disagreed with him?

As she reached for the door handle, his hostess reminded him once more that he was not to speak once inside. Eager to discover what awaited him—dream or no—he nodded his acquiescence and entered.

He was met by a feminine gasp from the other side of the room—where the bed was located, presumably. Locating the aforementioned chair with his knee, he threw off his cloak and mask and removed his clothes. Cool air caressed his naked flesh, but he wasn't cold—they must have warmed the room earlier, then put a curfew over the fire.

Reaching out, his fingers touched thick, flocked wallpaper.

This room must be right in the middle of the building, as there was no light at all. But he didn't need to think about that. The dream—or the reality—was about to get even better. As he made his way toward where he assumed the bed must be, a delightful aroma piqued his senses.

As he padded across the floor, his bare feet sank into the deep-piled carpet until his knees met a barrier of wood—the bed. He could hear the woman's rapid breathing—she sounded anxious. This ought to be a time for speech, for discussion, and reassurance. But he was a man of his word, and he'd promised to remain silent. If he was going through with this, his body must do the talking.

Locating the edge of the bed, he perched on it and ran his hand over the coverlet. She was already underneath, which presumably meant he'd missed out on the pleasure of undressing her. Why? What did she have to hide?

Nothing really mattered, though, did it, in this sensuous dream which had so much to offer? Climbing in beside his hidden companion, he drew the sheet over them both and reached for her.

By Jove—not even a nightgown! She was gloriously, unbelievably, naked. How did one begin when such a delicious treat was, as it were, handed to one on a plate? Especially when words were not permitted. He ought to begin slowly, and make sure to enjoy every moment.

Moving his hand to where he expected her face to be, he located and caressed her cheek, then pushed his hands into her loosened hair. It felt rich, heavy, and soft, and he was seized by the urge to bury his face in it. His manhood twitched in anticipation—but he must proceed with caution. First, he needed to make her happy. He could worry about himself later.

Brushing his thumb across her cheek, he heard her soft intake of breath and hoped it was pleasure rather than dislike. He moved his thumb down to her lips and traced their rich fullness, enjoying the delicate bow of her upper lip. She wasn't smiling, alas—was this nothing more than a business transaction for her? Now that he had committed himself, he intended to make it so much more.

He kissed her gently, teasingly. No response. Was this woman not used to being kissed? He touched his mouth to hers again and nuzzled behind her ear. A delicious scent thrilled his senses. It was nothing he recognized—not rose, not lilac, nor lavender. There was something musky and exotic about it.

Perhaps his wife-to-be was exotic too. The idea fired his blood. Warming to his work, he licked the rim of her ear, then nibbled gently on the lobe, and tugged at it with his teeth.

She exhaled the briefest of sighs—which he took to be a good sign. Was she as aware of the places where their naked flesh met as he was? She didn't shy away from him, so he edged closer, increasing the contact. Gods! Was that the press of a breast against his chest? It was firm but unbelievably soft. Surely, he was the luckiest of men!

He went to brush her lips again and met the tip of her nose. Smiling, he chuckled, then kissed her nose deliberately, and then her cheek, her temple, and finally, her mouth again. His free hand tangled in her hair, maintaining a rhythmic stroking to soothe her into accepting him.

Curse the fact that he was sworn to silence! He couldn't ask her what she wanted, or what she would permit. Making love to a stranger in the darkness was more intense than he could ever have imagined, and he needed all his concentration. He was having to battle the soporific laziness that kept threatening to steal over him, the result of whatever he'd unwittingly drunk.

He let out a soft sigh, then sought the mystery woman's mouth again. This time, there was some movement, and he increased the pressure. How could he make her kiss him back? He let out a soft moan of pleasure, as if her lips were the most wonderful thing he'd ever tasted, and thought her mouth smiled against his.

He turned his attention to her ear again and was relieved when she turned her head a little, giving him more access to her neck. Distracting her with a series of nibbled kisses down toward her shoulder, he moved his hand to her waist, and let it rest there, his fingers pressing gently against her side—not demanding, just comforting. As soon as his lips reached her shoulder, he moved back up to her ear again and repeated the process.

She sighed and shifted against him.

He stroked her hip, gently, and then harder. Perhaps this time, when he sought her mouth, she would kiss him back. Yes! She was responding, moving her lips over his as if exploring them. How much experience had this damsel had? Was she a virgin, or an experienced widow? Or even an *in*experienced one.

He could feel his interest piquing, his manhood rising in anticipation.

But it was too soon—far too soon. He pulled away a little but kept his mouth firmly on hers. How he longed to feel her beneath him, the full length of their bodies touching! What must he do to make her feel the same?

She seemed to be distracted by his kiss—her mouth was opening now, and her tongue darted out to meet his. He deepened the kiss, his hand stroking lightly across her breast, stalling briefly against her erect nipple, before moving to her shoulder again.

The way she lay rigid on the bed, like some wooden doll, perturbed him. She responded to him, yet she didn't hold him. He was used to more participation on the woman's part. He touched her breast again, and caressed it tenderly, then stroked her face. Her skin was smooth, and he explored her face with a light, deft touch. Yes, she was younger than he'd expected, but how young, he couldn't tell. Her nose felt exactly the size that a nose should be. Her mouth was exactly the right shape, her ears had the correct curve, and her eyes . . . if only there were light, so he could see the color of her eyes! He kissed her eyelids in a loving salute, before returning to her lips again.

Maybe it was time to tease her. Pulling back, he let the cool air flow between their bodies. She'd miss his warmth and want him back. After a moment's stillness, her hand touched his elbow, and awareness shot through him. The joy of her response, the power of that touch! There were other places he needed her touch, but that would, alas, have to wait. He was the master here—he had to control both himself and her. *For the time being.*

He rolled her onto her side, facing him. Much better—this felt more like it. He brought her hand to his lips in a tender salute, then kissed each one of her fingertips. Her little fingers felt slightly crooked and he adored the fact that she wasn't perfect—because perfect would have been dull.

She moved against him then, her interest awakened. He followed another slow, languorous kiss with what must have seemed like a chance touch on her breast and her nipple. Then he drew her close, and closer still, until the whole, hard length of him pressed against her.

A shudder ran through her—desire, he hoped. He stroked her back, feeling and appreciating every expanse, every curve until the goosebumps rose on her flesh, and her nipples hardened against his chest.

Kissing her again, his hand trailed across the dip of her waist and the swell of her bottom. She was a fresh peach, sensuous and luscious, and he longed to taste her.

When her hips pushed against his, he knew a moment of pure, masculine triumph. He rolled her onto her back again, and she went willingly, but still, her hands did no exploration of their own. He pushed aside his disappointment—there would be plenty of time in their life together for him to teach her what she might do to please him, and in doing so, please herself.

Leo discovered that he was grinning like an idiot—just as well it was dark! This was the best thing that happened to him in years—he couldn't remember when he'd last felt so happy. He'd vowed to be celibate after the loss of Elinora, thinking it a fitting sacrifice not to tarnish her memory by allowing any other woman into his heart.

Ah, Elinora. He paused and hung his head. What would she have thought of this high-stakes gamble? She'd tell him to go straight out and sober up, have a cold bath and stop being a fool.

He *was* being a fool! Who knew what manner of trap he'd stumbled into? If only he could clear his head—but his blood was thundering around his body in a fresh onslaught of lust, and it was impossible to think straight.

It was at that moment when his resolve hung in the balance that his lover's hands reached for him and tugged gently at his hair. She wanted another kiss. Well, he was a gentleman, and who was he to refuse a lady's request? He lowered himself down to her, allowing her to feel some of his weight, and helped himself to her mouth again, driving in more deeply, possessing her more thoroughly. Finally, wonderfully, she began to move beneath him, that almost-unconscious and inviting pushing of the hips.

He smiled. That little pause had made her anxious and forced her to enter the game. He decided to torment her more. He brushed his cheek against one breast, laved an erect nipple with his tongue, and was rewarded with a gasp. He pulled away, stroked the sides of her breasts, then gave the other nipple the same treatment. She sucked in another sharp breath.

It was the hardest thing of all, to pull away again, and wait for her response. But eventually, her hands were on his body again, feeling their way down his flanks, exploring every muscle, every sinew. Then she pushed at him again in mute demand.

This time, he took a nipple in his mouth and sucked gently, grazing it carefully with his teeth. His kiss swallowed her gasp. When she pushed against him urgently and her hands pressed into his flesh, he knew he was winning.

Her hands felt their way up his neck, forced themselves into his hair, then explored his neck and the muscles of his shoulders. He groaned, and raised himself, nudging her legs with his knee. She immediately parted for him.

My word, could she be ready for him so soon? He stroked her crotch, and she let out a shuddering sigh. Then her hands bit into his shoulders—she wasn't ready to relinquish power to him just yet. Forcing down his excitement, he paused once more, then lowered his head to bestow a kiss on the exquisite silk of her mound. He waited, repeated the gesture, then waited again.

If only she would touch him now! She *must* be able to feel his pendant manhood brushing against her belly. But if it was too soon for her, he understood. Pleasure was infinitely more delicious when one had to work for it.

He laid his hand between her legs and let it remain there, allowing her to get used to the feel of him so close to her entrance. Then he deployed his finger, returning his mouth to hers to gauge her response. The bucking of her hips told him all he needed to know, as did the flow of hot moisture between her legs. She was ready for him. Could he endure waiting a moment longer to claim her for his own?

He pushed against her opening, gently, slowly, inexorably. She was tight—oh, so tight! He would have to take his time, but that made the ultimate reward all the more precious. If only he could speak! He would tell her how divine she was, how wonderful she felt to touch, to smell. That exotic scent she wore was making him dizzy—or was it just the delirious happiness that washed over him?

Now he was inside, and he could feel the welcoming warmth of her body clenched around him. Was any sensation ever as exquisite as this one? Men might drink, fight, take opium, and race horses, but there was no experience, no sensation, as all-encompassing, as miraculously satisfying, as joining with a woman. He pressed deeper, withdrew, then pushed in again.

She had wrapped her legs around him now, giving him full access to her soft core. They were no longer two separate beings, but one, squeezing, pushing, driving each other higher and higher. He wanted to make this last. He needed to prove to her that he was no selfish lover, that he could be the best husband any woman could want in her bed.

But of course, his body had its needs, and he'd deprived himself for too long. He pressed in again, and again, and increased his speed, relishing the friction, the hot moist contact between their bodies, his hardness and her softness, complete opposites coming together to create one ecstatic whole.

He should pull out—now was the moment to withdraw. He attempted to disentangle himself from the woman wrapped so tightly around him, but suddenly she had him in a bruising grip, urging him on and refusing to let go.

For a dizzying moment, his willpower hung upon a knife edge. Then, accepting that this was what she wanted, he permitted himself a glorious release, unable to prevent the impassioned moan that escaped his lips. She made small sounds of her own, gasping, breathing rapidly, sighing, and whimpering as her head moved from side to side. It was almost as if she were surprised by her response, as if she'd never experienced such ecstasy before.

He supposed he should be proud of himself. His face broke into a self-congratulatory smile. How he wished for light, so she could see how gratified he was, how thrilled and delighted to have made her his. And he needed to know that he'd pleased her.

His body relaxed into the deep calm he always felt after such intimacies, and he rolled onto his back, pulling her with him, and rested his chin against her hair. Normally at a time such as this, sweet words would be exchanged, and vows of everlasting love declared. But they were forbidden to speak, he couldn't see his lover, and it was killing him. So, he held her close, stroked and soothed her, and made wordless sounds of comfort and reassurance.

Later, when he was sure she must be asleep, he eased away, pulled the covers up to her shoulders, and felt his way back in what he thought must be the direction of the door. It was high time he looked upon the face of the woman he had claimed for his own in the most fundamental way possible. Forgetting that he was still naked, he flung open the door, allowing flickering lamplight to flood the room.

And was immediately gripped around the neck by a strong arm while a bag was forced over his head.

Chapter Six

Araminta awoke. She stretched lazily, luxuriously, then opened her eyes.

The room was still dark—good. She had no wish to leave the bed yet—her body thrummed with pleasure still, and she reached for the man who'd gifted her such ecstasy throughout the night. She'd never known it before, and the idea that she might actually have the same joy repeated in the marriage bed was as heady as strong wine.

She felt for her lover, but there was no warm, powerful body beside her, no head upon the pillow. As she sat up in shock, she realized what had woken her—there was a ruckus in the corridor outside. It sounded like a fight, with curses, grunts, and bumps. Alarmed, she felt around for a lamp, but there was none.

Where were her clothes? She couldn't face danger naked. Gathering a sheet around her, she padded to the door, and at the same time, a man shouted, "Get your hands off me. Don't you know who I am?"

His voice was strangely muffled. Had someone been trying to break into their room, and was he being restrained by one of Mrs. Dove-Lyon's veterans? For a brief moment, she feared it must be one of her husband's relations, come to deny her the opportunity of taking over Forty Court.

The voice came again, and this time it was clear as a bell. "I wish to see Mrs. Dove-Lyon at once! You cannot treat a peer of the realm so shabbily!"

Her fear turned to dread. Oh heavens! She *knew* that voice—it was Lord Aylsham.

Scuttling back in the direction of the bed, she banged her knees painfully on the edge, then flung herself under the covers, fighting back tears. What was *he* doing outside? Oh, to be discovered thus by *him!* Aylsham's opinion of her was low enough already, but if he knew what she'd just done, he'd be appalled. He'd be sure to spread the word and ruin her reputation. He wasn't the kind to let sleeping dogs lie.

After all, she *had* dared to confront him, to stand up to him, and if he were the kind of man to have a resentful nature—which she suspected he was—he would revel in publicizing her downfall to all his cronies. She was finished!

Before she could work out what to do, the door opened and she froze, hoping that nothing of herself was visible.

"You may come out now, Lady Lamb. Everything has quietened down." Mrs. Dove-Lyon's voice.

Araminta let out an enormous sigh of relief. "It sounds as if there's been a battle outside."

She peeped out from under the covers as light filled the room from the widow's lamp.

"Yes. That was your husband-to-be, who urgently wanted a glimpse of your face. But that was not part of the plan. Obviously, I intend to introduce the pair of you a little later, under more genteel circumstances. Don't worry—he'll be taken away and bathed while we refresh his clothes. Then, we'll give him a decent breakfast. By the time we proceed to business, his temper will have cooled."

Lord Aylsham had bedded her? This couldn't be happening! It was some kind of sickening nightmare. She shook herself, but nothing changed. She was awake and in complete shock, and a heap of gentleman's attire lay on a chair near the door, testament to the fact that she wasn't dreaming.

There had to be some mistake. It couldn't possibly have been Lord Aylsham murmuring sweet sighs in her ear, it couldn't have been *him* making love to her so tenderly, so passionately. He was the last person in the world who'd agree to marry her when he knew her identity. And she could *never* agree to marry him, the self-righteous, implacable, objectionable fellow!

Her shoulders sank. So much for a marriage bed made in heaven. Her only hope was that they'd conceived a child. But would that plan work? Horatio's cousin was more worldly than she and had contacts and easy access to funds. Wouldn't she be safer with a husband as well as a child, a husband with the power and status to protect her?

But . . . not Lord Aylsham. Never *him*. She felt sick.

"Can I get dressed now, please?" She needed time to work out what she was going to do.

"But of course. And you must breakfast, too. I'll have some brought in here. What shall I order for you?"

There was a self-satisfied note in Mrs. Dove-Lyon's voice. The proprietress of the Lyon's Den apparently thought she'd secured a successful outcome. She couldn't be further from the truth.

"A little frumenty, perhaps?" She ought to have *something* to give her strength.

Mrs. Dove-Lyon scooped up the pile of gentleman's clothing and left the room. Shortly thereafter, a female servant appeared and helped Araminta to dress. This was a relief because she didn't feel able to dress herself. Her limbs were weak, and her fingers trembled. She was horrified at discovering the identity of her superlative lover.

This must be the very opposite of what Psyche had felt on learning that her monstrous husband, Cupid, became a handsome, golden-haired man at night. In Araminta's case, her lover had become a monster, and unlike Psyche, his disappearance left her with no desire to track him down to the ends of the earth. She had every intention of running—swiftly—in the opposite direction.

Having washed, dressed, and eaten a little frumenty, she felt more able to face the awkward conversation ahead of her. By the time Mrs. Dove-Lyon swept back into the room, her response was prepared.

"Are you ready to meet your husband-to-be?"

"No. My apologies, ma'am, but I've changed my mind. I no longer wish to marry—I'll find another solution to my problems."

Mrs. Dove-Lyon, who'd seated herself on the edge of the bed, stiffened.

"Did the man not please you?" There was ice in her tone.

Araminta couldn't lie about *that*. She wished she could. "He did. Very much so."

"Then what's the matter? You've been married before, and you know what relations are like between a husband and wife. Surely what you experienced last night was an improvement? If not, I'm seriously mistaken about the gentleman I chose for you."

Mrs. Dove-Lyon knew how Lord Aylsham performed in bed? Araminta's jaw dropped.

"No, not *that* way—I was a happily married woman. But I knew the gentleman's first instructor in the art of love—she's still a good friend of mine."

Araminta fought the urge to learn more. It was time to put an end to this scheme. Mrs. Dove-Lyon needed to know there was no hope whatsoever for any future with the man she'd chosen.

She took a deep breath. "Can I assume that nothing said in this room will go any further?"

After the briefest of pauses, her black-draped companion nodded. "As I may have mentioned, discretion is my watchword."

Despite this reassurance, Mrs. Dove-Lyon was clasping her hands so tightly, the knuckles were white. She was furious but trying to hide it.

Araminta forged ahead. "I heard the man's voice. I know who he is, and we're already at loggerheads. I can't see any way of amending matters between us."

There was another pause, and not for the first time, Araminta wished desperately that she could see the expression behind that concealing veil.

"I think you'll find that if you have spent a glorious night in a gentleman's arms—which you both enjoyed—it'll be far easier to build bridges." Mrs. Dove-Lyon relaxed her hands, warming to her subject. "You may not be aware of it, since it has not been your own experience, but many a tiff betwixt husband and wife is amended in the bedroom. I'm certain that once he knows your identity, the earl will do everything he can to amend the quarrel between you. At least meet with him, and see what can be salvaged."

The lady tilted her head, and Araminta felt her direct stare, even through the barrier of her veil. "Assuming you're correct about your lover's identity."

If only the woman would stop using that word! Every time she said 'lover', a hot shaft of excitement pulsed through Araminta's body.

She cleared her throat. "It's Lord Aylsham, is it not?"

"Ah." Mrs. Dove-Lyon nodded. "You weren't meant to know just yet. My apologies—my plans are normally carried out without a hitch. However, let me assure you that I've done my research most thoroughly, and I *know* he'll make you an excellent husband. When it comes to matchmaking, I'm seldom wrong—almost never, in truth. Do you understand? You must put your differences aside and move forward. Shall I call him in?"

Araminta had already overheard his lordship's anger at being accosted outside the bedroom door. She had no wish to arouse *that* beast again.

"Forgive me. I appreciate that you've done your best under the circumstances, but the seas will run dry before I choose to share my life with Lord Aylsham. I swear—I shall say nothing of this to anyone, so there'll be no doubt cast on your skills as a matchmaker. I'll shoulder the blame—had I told you Lord Aylsham was anathema to me, of course, you would never have chosen him."

The set of Mrs. Dove-Lyon's shoulders suggested she didn't agree, but that was of no importance. A thrilling idea had flashed across Araminta's mind. Maybe she could live with one of the *other* two gentlemen, the blond-haired fellow, or the mousy one.

Perhaps not. The Lyon's Den wasn't a shop window, where one purchased lovers to give one pleasure in bed. The bargain she'd made with Mrs. Dove-Lyon had misfired. It would be better to break it and risk no further mistakes.

"I'll pay what I owe. Then let us say no more of this."

The other woman got to her feet. "With respect, Lady Lamb, I think you're making a terrible decision. You're missing an opportunity few women in your position ever have. I can assure you that, in time, Lord Aylsham will dote on you, and will lay his heart—as well as his body—at your feet. Marriage to him would solve your financial difficulties, as well as his, by securing you the Lamb estate. I would therefore advise you to take some time to consider the matter—you may have three days' grace. If at the end of that time, you haven't changed your mind, any connection between us will be at an end. I'm a businesswoman, but I understand that occasionally the client does not want to take my advice. In the event that you fail to see reason, I'll only take half of my fee."

Well, that was something, she supposed. Every penny must be scrimped and saved if she and Belinda were going to be thrown out of their home. Horatio's cousin Thomas would never allow them to remain there—he had a shrewish wife who controlled him utterly and a legion of demanding children. He'd never had any time for her or

Belinda—they'd have to rely on their own resources.

"Is Aylsham still in the building?"

"Of course, he is. He's most keen to see his future bride. Two of my servants have black eyes as testament to his eagerness—and the power of his arm. However, we have a ladies' entrance for a reason. You can be smuggled out that way while we detain the earl. But as I said, you have three days in which to change your mind. It's not in my best interests to tell him you won't have him, but I'll find a way to stall him. I *did* warn him there might be a possibility of rejection, but apparently, he can't bear the idea of any stain on his honor. Go now. Good day to you."

Thus dismissed, Araminta stuck her bonnet on her head and pulled the veil down, then scurried out of the Lyon's Den. As she made her way along the street, she avoided looking up at any of the windows, lest Aylsham happened to glance out and recognize her as the irksome Widow Bellamy.

Thank goodness she'd escaped! It would've been awful to come face-to-face in the room where their union had occurred and make the discovery *then*. He would doubtless have had some vile, vicious words to say to her.

As she hailed a passing hackney carriage, tears pricked at her eyes. She'd been despoiled by her enemy—how was she ever to get over it? Only . . . her enemy had given her the most amazing night of her life. She was horrified to admit it, but Lord Aylsham's touch had awakened a voracious beast inside her. How was she to cope with the future, knowing she might never experience such ecstasy again?

CHAPTER SEVEN

LEO SAT FUMING behind his desk, his mind assaulting him with unpleasant memories of the Lyon's Den. Two days had passed and he still hadn't calmed down—it was as well Roland was out of town at the moment, or that young man would have borne the full brunt of his brother's ire.

Leo had never been so humiliated in his life. He'd always been a very private man, so to be accosted and restrained in such a notorious establishment, whilst completely naked, was something he wouldn't forgive for a very long time. Was his jealously-guarded good reputation now at stake? Had the night of passion with the alleged heiress been worth it? Unfortunately, despite the dent to his pride, he rather thought it *had* been.

He'd kept the lid on his temper—there had been no point making the situation worse. As soon as his assailants had overcome him, he'd been thrown into a bath before being reunited with his clothes. Then, he'd been given breakfast and subjected to a ruffled-feathers-soothing monologue from Mrs. Dove-Lyon, who never once lifted her veil.

That accursed Mrs. Bellamy had done exactly the same thing. Didn't women appreciate how infuriating it was not to be able to see their facial expressions? It was bad enough when men concealed themselves in identical clothes and masks, as they had that night. If it hadn't been for Roland cajoling him—and very possibly blurring his judgment by adding powerful substances to his glass—Leo would have walked out of the Lyon's Den at the earliest opportunity.

Not for an instant had he stopped thinking of that night in the mystery woman's arms, and the encounter with his flesh-and-blood Venus had taken on a dreamlike quality. Why had no one been prepared to reveal her identity? He'd begged, he'd blustered, and even tried to bribe Mrs. Dove-Lyon into giving up his lover's name.

But apparently, the final decision lay with Venus herself—and as he'd heard nothing, he must assume she'd found fault with him. This was a monumental affront to his masculinity. Was it wrong of him to imagine that any normal woman would be *eager* for a repeat performance of that night?

He hung his head. Yes, it probably was. Mrs. Dove-Lyon had said that he'd be introduced to the woman with whom he'd spent the night, and whom he was expected to marry, within three days at the most. Today was the second day, and his naturally pessimistic nature couldn't envision any successful outcome.

A nasty thought had wormed its way into his mind. Someone had just played the most unpleasant trick on him—soon his name would be on the tongues of all the tabbies or besmirched in anonymous letters to the newspapers. He'd slept with a malicious whore, had been sold the most ridiculous Banbury tale, and would be the laughingstock of London for months.

One way or another, he had to stop obsessing about it or go completely mad.

His chair scraped roughly against the floorboards as he thrust up from behind his desk and stomped out the door. It was exercise time in the yard, and one of the teachers was putting the older children through their paces—although, they were mostly so small still, the exercises were more of a romp. The babies had been brought outside to enjoy the fresh air too, but most of them preferred to slumber in their cots.

As soon as he stepped out into the watery April sunshine, there was a loud chorus of greetings, and the next moment, he found himself knee-deep in little children, vying with one another to hold his hand or cling onto his breeches. He picked up the tiniest of them and swung the boy onto his shoulders.

"Will you be a horse, Lord Aylsham?"

"For you, Patrick, I can be anything."

"Shall we have a race?"

This was a game the children had played before, and they loved taking it in turns to ride upon his shoulders. The teacher, Miss Brent, stood to one side and allowed him to take over the "lesson." Its main purpose was to tire the children out ahead of supper, which he could do just as well by racing around with them.

It took a while for everyone to pair up as horses and riders. It didn't matter who rode with whom—there would only ever be one winner. That would be *him,* on account of his longer legs, and the glory would go to his current jockey, Patrick. But there were no hard feelings about their unfair advantage—there would be more races, and every child would get a turn on his back.

It was a relief to gallop up and down the hard-packed clay of the yard, tiring himself, and giving him something to think of other than the smoldering night he'd spent with his mystery lover.

"This will be the final race!" he shouted, then let out a whoop and hurtled with his current rider toward the finish line. He still had enough energy to beat off all opposition and enjoyed a round of riotous applause from the foundlings as he gently lowered his jockey to the ground.

Breathless, tousled, and bent double with his hands on his knees, Leo discovered that the teacher and the babies' nurses weren't the only adults in the exercise yard. He was looking at the hems of two gowns, one black, the other, an attractive dove-grey.

He stood up swiftly, straightened his cravat, then froze. It was a moment before he found the breath—or the will—to speak.

"Mrs. Bellamy. I see you have returned. With reinforcements, if I'm not much mistaken." His tone was cold.

The young lady wearing the dove-grey, who was *not* veiled and was striking-looking, hurried forward. "Oh, sir, please do not desist. We have no wish to spoil the children's fun. Indeed, I would love to join in."

Her expression of earnestness took the wind out of his sails. She was charmingly blonde—not that he ought to be swayed by that kind of thing—and the appeal in her moist eyes was hard to resist.

"I'm afraid I don't have the honor of knowing your name, Miss . . . ?"

Mrs. Bellamy stepped forward. "This is my sister, Miss Belinda Bellamy. Do you think she might remain with the children while we talk?"

He could easily resist any request of Mrs. Bellamy's, but her sister was another matter entirely. "Their exercise time is nearly over, is it not, Miss Brent?"

"I wouldn't mind some help with getting them to untie their outdoor shoes when we go back inside. If Miss Bellamy doesn't mind."

Leo nodded, then glared at the veiled woman in front of him. "Still incognito, Mrs. Bellamy?" he hissed as he showed her into the office. "Or is Miss Bellamy your sister-in-law rather than a blood relative?"

"If I thought revealing my identity would make any difference to your opinion of me, or my designs, I would gladly do so."

His interest was piqued in spite of himself. She seemed like a changed woman today, but his mind failed to comprehend what it was about her that might be different. They were still enemies and he meant to give her no ground.

"Pray, take a seat. I must tell you, however, that whilst your generous donation has been gladly received, I'm still not letting you adopt a baby."

His companion paused before taking her seat. "But I have given you no money. Of that I'm certain."

"Indeed?" If she was being honest with him, it was most puzzling. He'd been positive that the one hundred thirty guinea donation he'd received this morning *must* have come from the so-called Mrs. Bellamy.

She shook her head vigorously. "It wasn't me."

"I suppose I may be mistaken. Although I would have expected anyone generous enough to give one hundred thirty guineas would want their generosity acknowledged. So, it definitely *wasn't* you?" He'd been so certain. *Most* peculiar.

She straightened, very deliberately lifted her veil and pushed it back from her face, then held his gaze.

In an instant, he forgot what he'd been meaning to say, and his heart drummed painfully in his chest. What was wrong with him? Why this new, unsettling excitement in her presence?

He took a deep breath and allowed himself to peruse Mrs. Bellamy's face. He was astonished at how young she was. Normally, a widow would be older, with that particular air that distinguished the married woman from the blushing virgin. He could see a marked resemblance between her and the damsel now helping Miss Brent with the children. The features were similar, the same small, pointed chins, large eyes, and abundant hair. But where Miss Bellamy—if that was indeed her name—was fair, her sister was dark. Mrs. Bellamy's locks were a deep chestnut brown, framing her face very pleasantly and complimenting her hazel eyes.

Her mouth, though unsmiling, was generous, but she wore a troubled expression, with a line between her eyebrows, as if she had a heavy burden to carry. There was an appealing blush highlighting her cheekbones.

Now that he had a face to look at, a real person in front of him, his enmity ebbed away. Curse it! He shouldn't allow himself to be affected so deeply by a pretty face.

"My name is Lady Lamb, sir. I'm the widow of the late Horatio Lamb. You may have heard of him?"

Leo pursed his lips. Yes, of course, he'd heard of Horatio Lamb—the man was notorious. A womanizer, gambler, drinker, and one who refused to back away from an argument, no matter how ridiculous it might make him seem. The fellow had considered himself one of the most dashing bucks of the *ton* and had convinced a few other people to believe it.

What it must have been like to be married to such a one, he could only imagine. A sliver of sympathy pierced his heart as he gazed at Lord Lamb's widow.

Leaning forward, he clasped his hands together. "Again, my condolences, madam. But I don't see how your revealing yourself changes anything, except to allow me a glimpse of the earnestness of your feelings. As I said before, the children are not for sale."

"I was considering offering to adopt a child, but this time, *not* making a donation. I fear that my previous offer of money made it seem like a payment, and that was what set you against me. Now that you know who I am, you know I can offer a child a good home."

"But you cannot offer that child a normal family, since you're a lady on her own. I'm sorry to be blunt about it, and I hope you understand that I'm not deliberately trying to distress you. But the constitution of the Foundlings' Hospital, which was established by my late mother, is quite clear that the children will either go into apprenticeships or be adopted into families where there are other children and both a father and a mother. This is the case with the babies, too. So, even if I wanted to, there's nothing I can do about the matter."

Lady Lamb stood and walked across to the window. "Then there is no hope for us."

He heard the catch in her voice, saw the drooping of her shoulders, and felt an unfamiliar stab of guilt.

He felt for his ring and twisted it around his finger. It was enshrined in the constitution that children could only go to complete homes. But could not the constitution be changed? Would the Board of Trustees be prepared to agree to such a proposition coming from him when he was already at odds with them? They wanted to sell the hospital and its land to Pargeter and remove the children to a cheaper site, thus raising more money for their care. But he knew the potential buyer was not to be trusted. No, he already had one battle on his hands—it was too dangerous to risk a second. He might end up losing on both fronts.

He joined Lady Lamb by the window, but she moved away, keeping her back to him.

"I'm sorry, your ladyship. It simply cannot be done." Glancing out the window, he watched as Lady Lamb's sister lifted a tiny child—Mary, he thought it was—and tickled her. The toddler laughed and tugged at Miss Bellamy's blonde hair. She was laughing, too, and the expression of adoration as she gazed at the little mite clutched at his heart. If he let them adopt a child, it would—at least until Miss Bellamy married—have a complete family. He now sensed that these two women could be relied upon to love any child that came to them.

"I can't suggest an alternative at the moment, but if you wish, I'll make inquiries and see if there's any other way you can adopt a child. How will that suit?" There were probably dozens of women in the boozing kens and bawdy houses of Whitechapel and St. Giles more than willing to sell their children. But he didn't like the idea of Lady Lamb going to such places.

"I would appreciate that, sir. Thank you."

Rather to his disappointment, she pulled her veil over her face before offering him her hand. It fit perfectly in his, but she snatched it away quickly, as if he'd burned her.

"We must go. Should you find a solution, we have rooms on Gordon Street. Just ask for Lady Lamb and Miss Bellamy. There's a large cherry tree opposite us, just coming into bloom. It looks like a huge pink candelabrum illuminating the street."

"I promise to make a particular effort," he assured her.

"In future I shan't insult your institution by offering you a large donation. In any case, what funds I was able to gather have now been spent."

Wisely, he hoped, although she didn't seem the kind of woman to be profligate. And now he knew who her late husband was, he applauded her for having survived marriage to such an appalling man.

Remaining studiously polite, Leo escorted her to the yard to collect Miss Bellamy, and then to the street gate where he lingered, staring thoughtfully at their retreating backs.

His mind was working rapidly when he finally strode back to his office, and he almost collided with the approaching beadle.

The man saluted and held out a letter. "This just came for you, your lordship."

"Thank you." Leo took it, recognizing the writing with a sinking heart. Another missive from Pargeter. Without ceremony, he broke the seal and discovered that the creature had increased his offer. It was still well short of what the land was worth, but the trustees had been jittery since his own donations to the hospital had dried up. It would be dishonest to conceal this new offer, and they were sure to leap at it.

He needed air. He stepped out into the yard, now empty of children, and gazed up at the sky. An early swallow swept overhead, harbinger of the summer to come. If the children were going to *have* to move, it was best to do it when the weather was good. But this was the only home they'd ever known—how would they cope with all the disruption?

He was going to have to sit down and work out what the relocation costs were likely to be and start hunting down another site. Which was the last thing he wanted to have to do. If only his ships had come in! He could have saved Mama's beloved project, which was now as close to his own heart as it had been to hers.

Raking his hands through his hair, he stared at the polished walnut surface of his desk, then gazed at the empty chair opposite his own, where the widowed Lady Lamb had sat. Was he too idiotically proud to take a woman's money? The Fates had been working against him for some time—until two days ago when he'd been offered a way out. Only a fool wouldn't take it. He must return to the Lyon's Den, and beard Mrs. Dove-Lyon in her lair. His marriage to the unknown Venus must take place, and her funds would save the Lady Aylsham Foundlings' Hospital, in the location and the form his mother had always intended for it.

He must cement that marriage before Pargeter began a major offensive. Knowing that snake's tenacity, it wouldn't be long before he showed his hand to the trustees. It was time for Leo Chetwynd, Lord Aylsham, to trample on his pride.

CHAPTER EIGHT

SHE'D SEEN HIM now, felt his presence, and heard his voice. Her body's reaction to him yesterday left no doubt in Araminta's mind that her superlative lover was Lord Aylsham. That a man like him could conceal such a capacity for tenderness and passion had been scarcely credible. But now that she'd seen him again, surrounded by children, no longer hiding behind the gloss of high society, she knew there was more to him than met the eye.

All the same, why couldn't her lover have been somebody else? *Anybody* else, in fact. Why did the man chosen as the perfect match for her turn out to be the one she most despised?

Ever since that unforgettable night, she'd felt exposed, vulnerable, and hollow. With her emotions ready to boil over at the slightest provocation, she had no idea how she'd maintained her equanimity on that visit to the Foundlings' Hospital. She'd been obliged to take Belinda with her for moral support—or to act as a distraction if one were needed.

Stirring sugar into her tea, she glanced across the breakfast table at her sister. Belinda had been unusually cheerful this morning, having evidently enjoyed being among the foundlings. The loss of her babe, even though its illegitimacy would have blighted her life, must have cut far deeper than Araminta could ever have imagined.

She'd never been in that position herself—she'd always assumed that Horatio must be impotent. Though she'd made discreet inquiries, there was never any hint that he'd put any of his mistresses in the family way. Although, of course, his mistresses would have known better than to take risks.

Whereas she, the respectable, widowed Lady Lamb, had taken every risk that night, and might even now be *enceinte*. If that were the case, it could solve all her problems—but there was no way of being sure, and she was running out of time.

Was marriage to Lord Aylsham the solution, after all? He must need money urgently, or he wouldn't have taken up Mrs. Dove-Lyon's challenge. Unless he'd been hoaxed. What if he refused her outright when he learned her identity? He might have done so already.

"Minty—you haven't touched your roll. I'll have it if you don't want it."

"I'm not hungry." How could she eat when her mind was in such turmoil? Not just her mind, in truth, but her whole body. She'd felt a javelin shaft of excitement when she'd laid eyes on Lord Aylsham, shamelessly admiring his tall, upright figure as he stood up from behind the desk and came to take her hand. She'd felt the full power of his touch then, and had been grateful for the gloves which stopped his touch from having its full impact.

She'd had to pull back so quickly, she feared she'd given herself away. Where had she found the courage to reveal her face to him? Maybe, deep down, she *wanted* him to know that it was she with whom he'd spent a night of passion. She *wanted* him to respond to her, to need her, to crave her again. But he'd given no sign of recognition.

He'd changed since she'd last met him in that office, though. He seemed softer around the edges despite being dignified and distant. And when she'd seen him with the child on his shoulders, her heart had given a peculiar lurch, and something melted within her.

No! She mustn't think of him as a potential husband just because of his male prowess—that way, madness lay. Or did it? If they both needed the same thing, could they not find some common ground? She flushed. They already *had*—that common ground was in the bedchamber.

"You're sickening for something, sister. At one moment you're pale, and the next you're red in the face as though you had a fever. *And* you won't eat. If Mother were alive, she'd tell you to go straight to bed, and send a hot toddy up after you."

"You're kind to care about me." It wasn't often that Belinda escaped her private prison of misery and became aware of the needs of others. Perhaps Horatio's death had changed her, too, and she now sensed that freedom was on the horizon. If only they could retain their home . . .

"Do you think, Belinda dear, you might like to visit with the children again?"

Her sister's eyes brightened. "Could I go and play with them like yesterday? Help them tie their shoelaces and apron strings? Carry the cots in and out of doors to make the most of the fresh air?" Then her face clouded. "But we can't go back there, can we? That horrible man wouldn't do what we wanted. I know you think I don't notice these things, but sometimes I do."

It would be splendid if Belinda could be found some occupation that involved little ones. Araminta sipped at her tea. Dared she face Lord Aylsham *again?*

"We might as well get *something* out of 'that horrible man,' as you call him. You said Miss Brent was very personable—perhaps she'd like an assistant in the classroom. I can't see Aylsham opposing that. You could help the children learn their letters, work on their arithmetic, or practice their handwriting. You were an able learner in the schoolroom, remember?"

Belinda tucked a lock of golden hair behind her ear and assumed a faraway expression.

"I was, wasn't I? Such a pity I fell in love with the lieutenant. He shouldn't have taken advantage of me, should he? And I shouldn't have let him."

Araminta leaped up and took her sister in her arms. "Don't even think of him. He's in the past and all that happened then is forgiven. Our future will soon be decided, and I see no reason why it shouldn't include you spending more time with little children if you enjoy their company so much."

If she *were* to become the bride of Lord Aylsham, as Mrs. Dove-Lyon advised, surely, he could not refuse Belinda the opportunity to work with the children? Being his wife would open many doors for them both, even the chance of a decent match for Belinda from amongst his acquaintance. Assuming that a man of such stubborn temper *had* any friends.

Araminta waited until she was sure Belinda wasn't going to burst into tears or throw a tantrum, then called for the carriage to be brought around.

"I'm going out for a little while, love. When I come back, I hope to have good news for you."

"Can I not come with you?"

There was a wheedling note in Belinda's voice. She had a bad habit of resorting to childlike behavior when she wanted something she didn't expect to get.

"Not this time. Next time, if you're good, perhaps." Araminta kept her voice firm and her expression serious. Thankfully, Belinda seemed to accept this bargain. Thankfully, too, she didn't notice the tremor of Araminta's fingers as she pulled on her gloves before hastening out of the door.

Now that Araminta had made up her mind to take this momentous step, she could brook no delay.

THE LONDON STREETS were choked with traffic—carriages jostling for position, people walking quickly with their heads down, and urchins running to and fro with brooms and placards. The air was filled with the sound of street vendors crying their wares and carrion birds bickering and scrapping over rubbish in dark alleyways.

Araminta gazed out the carriage window at the busy scene. With each minute that passed, she feared her courage would desert her—it was only the concern that her coachman would think her eccentric that stopped her turning tail and heading back home. She must delve deep into her inner reserves and put on a show of bravado, no matter how she felt. She was going to accept marriage to Lord Aylsham, and Mrs. Dove-Lyon would tell her how it was to be achieved.

Leaving the carriage a couple of blocks away from Cleveland Row, she drew her veil over her face and headed determinedly toward the blue-painted building which housed the Lyon's Den. So intent was she on speed, that she hadn't noticed another person heading for the very same building. Before she could check her step, she'd run full-tilt into him.

"Oh, forgive me—"

The words died on her lips. She stared up at the man who'd caught her, steadying her in his firm grip.

Lord Aylsham! What appalling luck to run into him before she'd had a chance to speak with Mrs. Dove-Lyon!

"Lord Aylsham." She cleared her throat. "Good morning."

He doffed his hat and sketched her a bow, stiff as an automaton at the fair, and clasped her hand to plant a kiss on the back of her glove. Expecting to be released immediately, Araminta froze when he held on and stared intently at her gloved hand.

"Good morning to you, Lady Lamb. I hope I didn't hurt you—I wanted to stop you falling. I know I can be like a charging bull when marching from one place to another. Or so my brother tells me." His voice died away.

Why was he not releasing her? Why was he studying her hand with such concentration? Of course—he was repulsed by the slight deformity of her little finger. She pulled away and shoved both hands behind her back.

Then, to her astonishment, Lord Aylsham leaned in, close to her neck, and inhaled deeply.

The clatter of horses' hooves died away and the regular hubbub of London ebbed into the background of her consciousness. She'd never felt someone's presence so powerfully, and it shook her to the core. Thus, it was with a stab of alarm that she looked up to see an expression of twisted fury on his face.

"It was *you,*" he growled. "*You* were my angel of the bedchamber, my Venus! That night—ah!" It sounded as if the man were in pain. "I refuse to believe that you and she are the same—and yet my body knows it! Your perfume, the shape of your fingers—the combination of both must be a rarity. Your presence here can be no coincidence."

He paused and pinched the flesh above the bridge of his nose, closing his eyes. "What a fool I've been! You couldn't get what you wanted by bribery, so you decided to use blackmail. Mrs. Dove-Lyon's your associate in this, with the connivance of Roland. I *knew* I should never have trusted him. Curse the day I ever set foot within those walls."

Of what, exactly, was he accusing her? How dared he? It wasn't she who'd lured him there—*that* had been at the design of others including, presumably, this Roland he'd mentioned.

"How can you be so ungentlemanly as to suggest such a thing! Do you want to make a scene in the street? Remember who you are, sir, and behave accordingly."

To her surprise, her words had the required effect. Aylsham straightened his shoulders and released her hand.

"Of course. We must discuss this with the spider at the center of this tangled web—the proprietress of the Lyon's Den. I want answers."

Araminta wouldn't mind a few answers herself. Such as, why was she feeling weak-kneed in the presence of her enemy? Where had she found the bravery to rebuke him, and why had he complied? Why had the discovery of her identity infuriated him so? It appalled her that he could believe such evil of her, that he could imagine she'd engineered the whole event in order to blackmail him.

His barbs had gone home, and they stung.

Her temper was close to boiling over, too, but she must take her own advice—it would ruin her reputation to be spotted disputing with this man in public. They must seek the brooding anonymity of the Lyon's Den.

Suddenly, as if in response to her wish, the familiar figure of Titan appeared.

He bowed. "Lord Aylsham, Lady Lamb. If you would be so good as to come this way, Mrs. Dove-Lyon would like to speak to you both."

"Mrs. Dove-Lyon must have a listening tube coming out onto the street, or be sitting in an upstairs window, peeping out from behind a curtain," Aylsham muttered.

"I believe she must," Araminta agreed.

Titan turned his back and led them toward an alleyway on the right-hand side of the building. Where were they going now—the tradesmen's entrance? She had no time to speculate further because Aylsham seized her elbow and escorted her in Titan's wake as if expecting her to make a run for it.

As if she would—she needed *some* hope to cling to. She'd come here to agree to a marriage that could bring many benefits—if only the objectionable Aylsham were prepared to stop behaving like a dunderhead.

They came to a halt, with Araminta shockingly aware of the heat of his touch. Titan had brought them to an extremely discreet entrance, which could only be accessed down a flight of stairs. Aylsham released her, and they walked in single file behind Titan along a convoluted series of stairways and corridors until, finally, they reached a room she'd seen before. It was the one in which she'd first encountered the black-clad, veiled, and imposing figure of Mrs. Bessie Dove-Lyon.

There she was, reclining on the chaise-longue as if she'd been there all morning, instead of spying on people in the street below. She didn't rise when Araminta and Aylsham entered but gestured them toward the sofa.

They were to sit together? Just like two naughty children being reprimanded by their governess. Araminta gulped. Sitting so close to Aylsham was *not* something she'd bargained on. Despite the chill of his demeanor, she couldn't ignore the heat of the strong, masculine body just a few inches from her own, nor could she prevent her eyes from straying to the man's long, muscular legs, or stop herself from remembering the assured, skilled touch of his fingers.

He held himself rigid and straight-backed, glaring at Mrs. Dove-Lyon. But when he opened his mouth to speak, she waved a dismissive hand at him.

"No doubt you have much to say, my lord, but please, let me speak first. Can I offer you any refreshment?" Mrs. Dove-Lyon glanced up at Titan, but Araminta and Aylsham spoke almost as one.

"No, thank you."

"I don't need anything, thank you."

Araminta exchanged a brief glance with her companion—was he thinking, as she was, that the refreshments at the Lyon's Den were not to be trusted?

The proprietress tilted her head in Araminta's direction. "Am I to assume that you have, after all, decided in favor of the gentleman I chose for you? The three days' grace I gave you is now up."

Araminta clutched her hands together. The man beside her was *not* going to like this. He wasn't going to like it one little bit.

"I have."

Aylsham drew in a breath, and his chest swelled. Swiftly, she laid her hand over his, and murmured, "Wait. Your wrath will achieve nothing here. When you're acquainted with the full circumstances, you may come to think better of me."

The breath hissed out between his teeth. He removed his hand from beneath hers but restrained himself from speaking.

Was it too soon to feel a sense of relief?

Mrs. Dove-Lyon's veiled face was now turned toward Aylsham. "When you came upstairs three nights ago, into the room where a naked woman awaited you, you were fully aware that the outcome of that event was to be a marriage."

"*Fully aware* might be stretching a point, madam. I think the drinks you serve here are rather stronger and more intoxicating than your customers believe them to be. But I admit, though it shames me to say it, that I had an expectation of becoming attached to an heiress. I have since had plenty of time to regret my folly."

Mrs. Dove-Lyon sniffed and gave a little toss of her head. "Please be honest with me, your lordship. When you made up your mind to visit the Lyon's Den today, what was your purpose?"

"I came to learn the identity of the woman I was supposed to be marrying."

"And now you know it. So, you can keep up your end of the bargain."

Araminta felt as if the weight of a thousand millstones were pressing down upon her. Her heart had forgotten how to beat, and she couldn't breathe. She didn't want him any more than he wanted her, but what other way was there to secure her future, and that of

Belinda?

Aylsham shot her a sideways look, then stared straight at Mrs. Dove-Lyon. "My 'intended' and I wish to be left alone. We need to have a full and frank discussion, the kind that should most definitely take place in private."

Araminta quivered and glanced sideways. Aylsham was continuing to stare down Mrs. Dove-Lyon. It was a shame no one could see the expression on that veiled face—it was becoming annoying, in truth. Araminta now understood why Aylsham had wanted her to unmask when she'd first visited him.

A battle of wills raged briefly between the earl and the Lyon's Den's proprietress. The earl won.

Rising from her chaise longue with queenly dignity, Mrs. Dove-Lyon exited the room. Aylsham collected a chair and placed it before Araminta, then settled down, and sat back. His pale grey eyes pierced her very soul.

Her cheeks heated, and she forced herself to stop imagining what he might look like naked, with candlelight flickering over his muscular contours. Having a sensible discussion whilst ignoring the demands of her imagination was going to be a struggle. Her accursed imaginings didn't diminish him in any way—though she still heartily disliked the man.

However, a few good points had penetrated the cloud of disapproval. He liked children, he'd been polite to Belinda, he'd put Mrs. Dove-Lyon in her place, and he was superlative in bed.

"I know what you're thinking."

She rather hoped he didn't. A blush suffused her entire body. Even her eyes felt hot.

"I doubt it."

"I'm seldom wrong. It just so happens that I'm thinking much the same thing. Damn you, woman."

With that, he pulled her onto his lap and kissed her.

Chapter Nine

Lady Lamb felt soft and pliant in Leo's arms, and as her exotic scent washed over him, his body caught fire. How easy it would be to kiss her senseless until he won her sweet surrender and tasted the incomparable delights of her flesh once again!

But that would be folly. They wanted each other—her response to his kiss told him that—but *he* wasn't after a mistress, and *she* needed more than a lover. There was too much at stake for him to let his passions take charge now.

He pulled away. "I hadn't meant to do that. Forgive me." Only—he found he couldn't release her.

She glanced at him, and he was surprised by the tenderness in her eyes. If only she would wrap her arms around his neck and push her fingers into his hair as she had that night. His throat went dry.

He really shouldn't keep her on his lap—it simply heightened his need. Besides which, anyone might burst in on them. Then he remembered what was rumored to go in the upstairs rooms of the building. The people who worked at the Lyon's Den wouldn't be easily shocked.

"I've been offensive—I apologize. I wasn't best pleased when I discovered your identity, Lady Lamb, and feared I'd been played for a fool. But if we're *both* to blame for the situation in which we find ourselves, we can only establish the fact through complete honesty. And I don't know about you, but I'm less than keen to unburden myself in front of Mrs. Dove-Lyon, even though she knows who we are and what we've done."

His Venus stirred in his lap. "I think I should return to my chair," she announced, prim as a schoolmistress.

At least *one* of them was being sensible. "Of course." He released her, with a mingled sense of relief and loss. "I shouldn't have importuned you like that, not when we have negotiating to do. Having established that you don't find me repulsive, let's progress from that point. Perhaps I should add that I don't find *you* repulsive, either."

She glared at him, affronted, and he chuckled. "I'm teasing you, your ladyship."

"I think we must be serious, sir, and put aside all consideration of that night we spent together in blissful ignorance of each other's identity."

As a gentleman, he could not. One did not plunder a young woman's treasures and then abandon her like some Viking after a raid. But he'd think about that later. For now, he needed to draw her out, find out what was behind her behavior, and—for the moment at least—give her the benefit of the doubt.

"After what has passed between us, Lady Lamb, I think we may progress to Christian names. Mine is Leo."

"You can call me Araminta. My sister calls me Minty, but I don't encourage it."

Minty Lamb. Yes, he could understand why it might annoy her. He must fight any urge to call her by that hurtful name. He must fight some other urges too. Devil take it! He needed a clear head. She'd think him an idiot if he didn't come to the point soon.

"If I tell you the reasons which persuaded me to do what I did, will you reciprocate? I don't want there to be any secrets between us. Especially if we are to go ahead and combine our resources."

Her hazel eyes were huge and troubled. She bit her lip, which inflamed him. He wanted to bite it too, to arouse the passion he knew was in her.

He ran a finger around inside his collar. "I come from an ancient family, Araminta, whose seat lies in deepest Norfolk. We made a fortune in the woolen cloth trade and rose to greatness. As you know, there's been an upsurge in cotton of late, and heavy competition within the cloth industry. So, I decided to venture into cotton and muslin and invested in three cargoes of the stuff. Alas, the ships I chartered have failed to make port and there's increasing concern that they may have foundered in a storm." He clenched his fists. It pained him to expose his folly, his stupid gamble, to her.

He forced himself to continue. "Therefore, I find myself in financial difficulties. But it's not only that which concerns me at present. There's also an issue with the Foundlings' Hospital. The place was so dear to my late mama's heart, but now I fear I can no longer comply with her wishes and keep it as it is. Desperate action is needed."

That sounded melodramatic—he didn't want her to think that *she* represented that "desperate action," even if she *did*. He went on to explain Pargeter's intention of purchasing the hospital for the land, and how the only way to stop him was to either buy the place himself or pay off the other subscribers.

"With so much at stake, sir, I'm surprised you refused my generous offer," she said after listening to his account. "It could have resolved your problems—but I suppose you were too proud to accept my money."

"Not exactly. Shall we call it a misunderstanding?" She was right—he *was* proud. But he had no wish to confess to any further failings. Her opinion of him now meant a great deal.

"It later occurred to me that the constitution might be changed, under certain circumstances, but I'm worried that I'm running out of time."

"Is there anything else you need to tell me?"

Did she mean to expose all his secrets? He wasn't sure he wanted to part with those yet. He lifted his chin. "If there's some likelihood we might be married, you need to know that I'm fit and healthy, have a London townhouse as well as an estate in the country, and my teeth are all my own. I have been married—" His voice caught, and he forced himself to continue. "I was married to Elinora, but childbirth stole both her and the babe from me. I have not felt complete since."

It was the first time he'd admitted openly that he was still grieving. Not even Roland was aware of it—perhaps he'd hidden it *too* well. Curious that he should confess his feelings so openly to a woman he barely knew . . .

"Would you wish to begin a family anew?" Araminta's face was tense, alert. This was clearly important to her.

"Of course. Every man needs an heir, and I have no expectation of my brother Roland coming to anything much—pray, don't tell him I said so! He can't decide what he wants to do with himself and ends up wasting time gambling with what remains of the family money. I'd far rather the Aylsham estates went to a child of mine than to *him*. He's a very personable fellow, I hasten to add, and I'm deeply fond of him. But he's feckless—there's no point making any bones about it."

Suddenly he became aware that he was revealing far more of himself than he'd intended to. It wasn't like him to speak so freely. What was there about this woman that invited confidences?

"I should like to meet him." Araminta's hazel eyes were earnest, and he found himself wishing she hadn't worn a veil the first time she'd come to him. If he could have seen her face, he would have seen the honesty there. And the beauty . . .

He was being idiotic. The current circumstance was exceptional—he mustn't give anything further away until he was certain she was to be trusted. And his heart must remain his own.

"Now it's *your* turn to explain why you approached Mrs. Dove-Lyon, and took such desperate measures to land yourself a husband."

She broke eye contact with him. "I don't wish to dwell on my marriage, but as you already know, I'm now a widow and childless. There was a clause in my husband's will which made it clear that I was only to remain at Forty Court if I produced an heir within the first five years of our marriage. However, the will was very poorly put together, because the lawyer who wrote it was, to put it politely, a bit of a toper. Strictly speaking, nowhere does it say that the heir has to be Horatio's—it can also be *mine.* Thus, I came to you in the hope of adopting a baby and passing it off as mine and Horatio's—that seemed at the time the best way to secure everyone's future quickly, for I also have my sister's interests at heart. I was then persuaded it would be better to marry again, and quickly, so I'd have the protection of a husband. It could be argued, due to the ramshackle wording of the will, that any child I had with that husband would still inherit."

She paused, and a tremor ran through her. For a brief instant, she appeared as if she was frightened she'd said too much. But he was feeling too hopeful now to pay it much heed. She was not the scheming monster he'd originally believed her to be.

"Adopting a baby would have been deceitful and wrong," she continued, "and I might have been found out in any case—Horatio's relations are grasping and imperturbable. I hope you never have to meet them. Particularly his cousin Thomas, who stands to inherit the most."

"I rather hope I *do.* I might have a word or two to say. They should be supporting the grieving widow, not trying to steal her home out from under her."

Araminta glanced up at him as if surprised to find him on her side. She was going to need a lot of convincing of his good intentions. Like her, he should acknowledge his mistakes and learn his lesson with good grace.

"So, having heard about the services offered by Mrs. Dove-Lyon, I took the money I'd planned to offer the children's home, and paid it to her instead, in return for which she promised to find me a suitable—and eager—husband."

She'd paid Mrs. Dove-Lyon? How appalling it was that a good woman should be in such dire circumstances! He decided there and then that he'd find a way to reimburse Araminta. Or shame the Lyon's Den proprietress into returning the money.

"May I ask what this devious matchmaker charges for her services?" He doubted that her costs would be reasonable.

Araminta flushed. "I'd rather not say."

"Please?" He needed to find out all he could about this affair, needed to ensure that whatever he was letting himself in for, it would be with both eyes open.

"Two hundred sixty guineas."

"I can see I've underestimated my own value. I didn't know fortune-hunting gentlemen were so highly prized!" His mouth twisted. "Curiously enough, I received an anonymous donation the other day, for exactly half the amount you mention." Surely, that was no coincidence?

"You think *she* might have sent it? I can't imagine why she would have done that. Unless it was her way of meddling, and making sure you sought me out because you imagined it was from me."

"But she must have known that setting us at loggerheads would not have progressed her matchmaking plan." Unless it was a salve to her conscience. If Mrs. Dove-Lyon *had* a conscience . . .

"I know. It's a puzzle."

"I'm concerned that you agreed to her methods." *Even though he'd enjoyed every last second.*

Araminta tilted her chin at him. "I'm surprised *you* agreed to them, especially as I can now see how easy it would be for either one of us to fall victim to blackmail. Anyway, I accepted before I fully understood what was expected. By that point, I was in so deep, I couldn't see how to dig myself out again. Mrs. Dove-Lyon was so very certain she'd found the perfect man for me—she gave me hope. I mean, she couldn't do a worse job of it than I did myself. I fell in love with Horatio Lamb, didn't I?"

The bitterness in her voice tugged at his heart. She'd had a rough ride, and he'd been less than sympathetic at the time.

"Did you have any choice regarding the gentleman who was to spend the night with you?" A leading question, and he'd surprised himself by asking it. Was he fishing for compliments?

"I did." She leaned forward, holding his gaze, her expression earnest. "I genuinely didn't know it was *you* though, I swear. There were three men, and you were the least foolish of them."

Rocking back in his chair, he let out a hearty laugh. "Now I know what is meant by being damned with faint praise!"

"I'm only telling you the truth."

"Of course." He twirled his ring, but when her eyes were drawn to the movement, he forced himself to stop. "So—now we both know where we stand. Your funds would be extremely useful to me in keeping the Foundlings' Hospital afloat since I can't put any more of the Aylsham money into it without selling the land that's vital to the estate's income. I can—I hope—be useful to *you* since we both know I'm capable of fathering a child."

What he'd meant to say died on his lips. What if he'd *already* fathered a child on her? It wasn't unheard of for a woman to become *enceinte* after a single mating. How could he risk Araminta giving birth to his child if he wasn't married to her? No gentleman worth the name would ever despoil a lady and then abandon her. Mrs. Dove-Lyon had known what she was about.

"I think this was meant to be." His words came out as a whisper. Heart thundering, he knelt at Araminta's feet and took her hand in his. "Araminta Lamb, would you do me the honor of becoming my wife?"

She gripped him with both hands and pressed her forehead against his knuckles. He could feel the tension emanating from her—was she about to refuse him? Impossible! It would make a mockery of everything they'd done so far. It would also *hurt*—far more than he could have believed.

"There's one more thing you need to know, Leo. If you marry me, and if I have a child, it must be given up into foster care immediately. Only that way can I retain control of Forty Hall and its income."

"What? *Why?*" Agony sliced through him. How could he let any child of his be taken away?

"My husband was determined that his heir would not be molly-coddled or smothered by affection. He felt it was character-forming to avoid such emotions—I imagine he thought I would be too loving a mother."

"There's no such thing." Leo's mind was in a whirl. He'd have no time to spend with his child, all because a drunkard had written up the last will and testament of a heartless villain? Elinora's image swam before him, and he remembered the vivid joy on her face when she'd found herself with child.

He could feel Araminta's gaze on him, heard her shallow breathing, and sensed her alarm at his silence. He'd already made his offer, despite not knowing all the circumstances—he'd hate himself were he to take it back. The past was done with. The future must always hold hope, otherwise, what was the point of continuing to exist?

"I'm sure we can work something out. Together. Lord Lamb's will may not be as immutable as you believe." He hoped he'd kept the doubt out of his voice.

Araminta let out a sob.

"No! It's impossible. I can't do that to you—not after all you've lost. I've made the most dreadful mistake. Don't follow me, I beg of you—we must never meet again. I'm so very, very sorry!"

Tearing her hand from his, she rushed from the room.

Chapter Ten

Any other gentleman would have realized that Araminta was doing him a favor by fleeing. But if the expression on Lord Aylsham's face was anything to go by, he was utterly disgusted. Or suffering from wounded pride. No matter. He'd get over this whole dreadful affair quicker than *she* would. Brushing the tears from her eyes, she glanced over her shoulder to see if he was following her. Correction—to make sure he *wasn't* following her.

There was no one there. Well, she couldn't blame him. No gentleman of his standing was going to chase out into the street after a woman, particularly not when the building he was exiting was the notorious Lyon's Den. Suddenly recalling her own situation, she flipped her veil down. There was no point in risking a scandal.

Yes, he should be grateful that she'd rebuffed him. He wouldn't want to give up a child any more than she would—she'd seen how much he enjoyed the company of the children at the Foundlings' Hospital. He cared deeply about them and about the enterprise. It wasn't just that he'd inherited it from his mama—it was close to his heart, something Araminta understood even better now she knew he'd lost a child of his own.

How could she do that to him, despite his noble protestations that he could deal with it, or find a way around it? Even if he had turned out to be just as detestable as she'd originally believed, he didn't deserve to be inveigled into a marriage where he'd be deprived of his own child.

Belinda wouldn't be happy if the baby were to be sent away, either. Oh, what an accursed, agonizing mess this all was! As soon as she reached the carriage, Araminta subsided gratefully into its dim interior, determined never to go near the Lyon's Den again—or Cleveland Row—or even this quarter of London.

She sighed and gazed unseeing through the window. She'd been pressured into the utmost folly and might not only hurt herself but everyone else into the bargain. Thank goodness she'd had the sense to call a halt before any more harm was done—just imagine the scandal she'd have created, marrying again so soon after Horatio's death! There had to be another way out of her dilemma—she just needed time to think.

There was a sudden rattle of rain on the carriage roof—an April shower. Glancing up at the grey sky, she found that the weather matched her mood perfectly. The only thing that would cheer her up would be to find Belinda in good spirits when she returned to their rooms in Gordon Street.

Her sister was in the doorway the instant the carriage drew up before the house. However, her expression was hardly encouraging. As Araminta stepped down, Belinda rushed out to meet her, her face pale and anxious.

Araminta lifted her veil and attempted a smile. "What are you doing outside? You don't have your shawl on, and it's raining."

"Oh, it will be done in a moment. Where have you been? We've been worried about you. A letter came—it must be important."

Araminta hustled her sister indoors and immediately called for tea. Then, after divesting herself of her bonnet and gloves, she picked up the letter from the hall stand and took it into the parlor.

She recognized the writing, and her heart jerked uncomfortably. "It's from Forty Court. I wonder what Mrs. Aldridge has to say to me?"

She'd hoped the Lamb estates had been left in good hands during her prolonged absence with the pregnant Belinda. The housekeeper and her husband, the steward, had reassured her everything would run smoothly, despite the recent death of their master. Were there financial issues? Problems with the planting at Home Farm, or sickness amongst the livestock? There was so much Araminta just didn't know how to manage, had never been *allowed* to manage. If only she'd returned from the Lyon's Den with a better outcome! Had she made a dreadful mistake in refusing Lord Aylsham's suit?

She forced herself not to open the letter until she and Belinda were seated by the fire, with a fortifying cup of tea each and portions of Cook's best currant cake. Then she read the missive through. Not believing her eyes, she read it again.

A cake crumb caught in her throat and she struggled to breathe. "How dare he!" she spluttered. "The infernal cheek of the fellow!"

"Drink your tea, Araminta. Don't eat and speak at the same time—our poor, dead Mama would not have approved."

Araminta made no comment. She dared not share this deeply unsettling news with her sister, lest the girl throw one of her sobbing fits.

"Would you mind terribly if we returned home, my dear?"

"What, leave London already? But we've only been here a little while. We haven't seen Vauxhall Gardens, the Royal Academy, or even Hyde Park yet. Although I understand it may not yet be the weather for it. But I have my new pelisse and my woolen mittens that you made me. I'm sure I would not catch a cold."

Thank goodness Belinda was focused on less weighty matters than their future security and comfort. "We'll visit again when it's warmer. But would you not like to return home, and feed the lambs, and help with the milking? There might even be a new litter of kittens from the farm cats."

Belinda's eyes brightened. "Is that what it says in your letter? I adore kittens."

"Yes, it is mentioned." Sometimes it was better to lie to Belinda than to tell her the truth. Out of the best possible motives, of course.

"What about the baby? Didn't we need one? And don't forget the orphans. I was hoping I could go and help with them. I'm sure Lord Aylsham would allow it if I asked him nicely."

The mention of Lord Aylsham brought back the memory of his face as Araminta had last seen it, right before she'd abandoned him. Had that stricken look *really* been one of wounded pride? Or had he felt her desertion more keenly than she imagined?

No, surely not. They barely knew each other—except in *that* way, of course, where they probably understood each other better than many married couples.

Her cheeks heated. "Pray, do not mention him."

"Have you come to blows again?"

"What makes you think we have *ever* come to blows?" Belinda didn't normally notice anything outside her own narrow purview.

"I'm aware of more than you imagine, Araminta. I just don't always know what to do about it—I'm so afraid of doing or saying the wrong thing. I have said, and done, many wrong things in the past, which I regret. Anyway, you don't answer my question."

"No—we have not had a fight." Quite the opposite, in fact. They'd come to a very good understanding, until her brutal revelation. "I just realized that it was probably better for him if I didn't trouble him anymore."

"You were always very thoughtful."

She'd always tried to be, but becoming the bride of Horatio Lamb had hardened her, and she was fighting to get back to the soft-hearted, compassionate person she'd been before.

"How long before you're ready to make the journey? Will you be able to leave today?" She knew Belinda was not to be hurried—it took her time to become accustomed to any change of plan.

"Could we make it tomorrow? I *so* need to wash my hair and curl it—this damp weather treats it very shabbily. And there's a tear in my traveling gown which I must mend. I know it isn't far to travel, but one never knows what might happen—a wheel could come off, and we might have to spend the night at a country inn, and I would hate to be seen not looking my best."

"What an imagination you have! I don't see us having any accidents between here and Forty Court—it's less than two hours' journey. And the roads are good."

"Only if it stops raining," replied her sister darkly. "But I'll go and fetch my mending now, while the light still lasts."

Araminta stared at the remains of her tea, and wished Belinda hadn't left so soon—she didn't want to be alone with her thoughts and her fears. The letter that had come, which would force her to go back to Forty Court far sooner than she'd planned, was from her housekeeper, announcing the arrival of an unexpected guest. It was none other than Horatio's odious cousin, Thomas Bilson. She'd have to return home to deal with him, and as she'd be arriving without an heir, Thomas would know immediately that Forty Court would soon be his.

In fact, he'd already made that assumption. Mrs. Aldridge had not felt it her place to refuse entry to the late Lord Lamb's cousin. Consequently, Mr. Bilson had installed himself in the master bedroom at Forty Court, and was, at the time of writing, making inquiries for a local surveyor and valuer. He considered himself already in charge and felt there was no way in which Lord Lamb's widow—or her sister—could justify remaining in a house they had no right to.

It was an open declaration of war.

CHAPTER ELEVEN

LEO MADE ANOTHER circuit of the wood-paneled parlor. Surely, Araminta should have been home by now? He'd been certain she couldn't be far behind him on his journey to Forty Court, and he'd ridden Caesar very gently. He'd already done Araminta an enormous favor, and he couldn't wait to tell her.

If only she would come!

He walked around the room again, glanced at the glass of sherry the housekeeper had brought for him, then stepped across to look out the window. No sign of the Lamb carriage. What if something had happened to her? It seemed unlikely, but to a man in his present state, every imagined action was fraught with peril, and he feared the worst.

He must fetch Caesar from the stable and return along the road. What if the carriage had overturned, or collided with another? He couldn't bear the thought of his Venus lying hurt somewhere. He bit his lip, relishing the pain, then sat down and grasped the sherry glass.

Its sweetness calmed him. Just a little. It wasn't like him to be so anxious and jumpy—he would never achieve what he had set out to do if he couldn't control himself. Glancing at the clock, he saw that he'd been here over an hour now. At least the initial part of his visit had been spent fruitfully and had made an ally of Mrs. Aldridge, the housekeeper. She'd rewarded him with a tour of the house.

Forty Court was pleasant enough, though truly ancient. The grounds were charming, and instead of the more modern style of ha-ha, the house was separated from the old deer park by a red brick wall and sequestered from the outside world behind a large pair of iron gates. The estate must be a reasonably profitable enterprise, judging by the number of animals he'd seen at pasture on his ride up the drive.

The house itself was built in the traditional Elizabethan E-shape, with a paved courtyard and multiple lead-paned windows which glittered in the sunlight. The public rooms were of a good size, and the old great hall was resplendent with stone and wooden carvings, as well as a minstrels' gallery. The attics were vast and ran around all three sides of the building.

Yet . . . there was something missing. The furniture and decoration had been completed in a hard, masculine style. There were no tapestries, no striped upholstery, no Chinese wallpaper, or ruched drapes. It was as if the house held no females whatsoever. Had Araminta not had long enough to put her stamp upon the place? Or had her husband refused her that privilege? Leo was already hating the fellow, and not just through jealousy.

At that moment, he heard horses' hooves and carriage wheels clattering across the courtyard. Anticipation lanced through him. Setting down his glass, he rushed to the window, just as the carriage halted before the main entrance.

Thank heaven! There was Araminta alighting, and apparently, quite unharmed. Miss Bellamy followed her and didn't seem any the worse for wear, either. There was rather a lot of mud sprayed up the side of the carriage, however. Horrible things, carriages. He had far rather travel by horse and put up at country inns wherever necessary. They were always the most entertaining places to be.

Araminta was coming in—he could hear footsteps in the hallway, and his heart somersaulted. No—he mustn't chase out to meet her—that would seem far too eager. Besides, he had no idea what his reception would be. Their meeting must happen in the privacy of the parlor, rather than in the hall under the eyes of all and sundry.

A murmur of voices was followed by an exclamation, then Araminta burst into the room.

"What on earth are you doing here, Lord Aylsham?" She frowned. "And where is my husband's cousin, Mr. Bilson, who I'm told was visiting here?"

It was as much as he could do not to close the distance between them and take her in his arms. But he had a bit of explaining to do and preferred her not to be angry when he did it.

"I threw him out on his ear. An objectionable fellow." He tried not to look smug. The removal of Mr. Bilson had been a minor coup, but enjoyable all the same.

Araminta's jaw dropped. "You threw him out?"

"Yes. He seems to have a proper respect for titles, and I gave him every inch of mine. I also informed him that I was your fiancé and that if he didn't leave immediately, there would be consequences he wouldn't find pleasurable. I understand that he meant to meet up with a surveyor and a valuer later, but I'm happy to deal with them on your behalf when they arrive."

Araminta collapsed into a chair, then drew off her gloves and dropped them to the floor. "You have more than made yourself at home, sir. I cannot believe your arrog—"

Before she could finish, or give him a chance to defend himself, Belinda cannoned into the room.

"Lord Aylsham! How lovely to see you!" She threw her arms around him and embraced him. He was still gaping in astonishment when she released him and glanced around.

"Have you not brought any of the orphans with you? I should've thought they'd love to come and play at Forty Court."

Leo was too busy drinking in the sight of Araminta, her cheeks flushed from the fresh air, her eyes bright with indignation, to take much notice of her sister. My, but his Venus was a beautiful woman. If only he could convince her that his suit was in earnest.

"Yes, Miss Bellamy. They probably would." He faltered, and his pulse quickened. Miss Bellamy's words had spawned an idea . . . but there were more important things to settle first.

"Belinda, please! This is not the way we greet guests, remember?"

The younger woman's shoulders drooped, and she looked more like a lost child than ever.

Araminta flushed guiltily. "But I'm sure Lord Aylsham will forgive you," she amended. "Won't you, sir?"

He nodded but continued gazing at her, his carefully-prepared speech all but forgotten.

"He does not seem too concerned about the social niceties, either," Araminta continued. "He is more than happy to invade someone else's home in their absence, and deal summarily with their relations, regardless of what the consequences might be."

That brought him back down to earth. So much for assuming he could please her by ejecting Mr. Bilson. She must understand, surely, that he'd felt obliged to remove the man. And that he wouldn't dream of leaving her alone to face the consequences—if, indeed, there were any?

If she didn't trust him, then he must make her.

"Miss Bellamy, you must be in need of refreshment. Why don't you call for some tea and see about getting your luggage brought indoors? No need to hurry—your sister and I have much to discuss."

Araminta shot him an inimical look as Miss Bellamy trotted out of the room.

He hastened to Araminta's side. "I thought it best that we speak in private," he explained, lowering his voice. "You left me so precipitously—you didn't even wait to hear *my* feelings about giving up a child into foster care. I beg you not to make assumptions about me when you know me so little."

The angry look faded. Araminta busied herself removing her bonnet whilst avoiding his gaze. He took the bonnet from her, set it down, and closed the door.

"I was concerned when I arrived so far in advance of you. Truly, I never meant to ambush you—I had fully expected you to be here already. Did you meet some misadventure upon the road?"

Why was he making small talk when they had far more significant matters to discuss?

"I don't know why you had to close the door to ask me about my journey, my lord."

"Call me Leo, please. There are things we need to talk over in private."

"Perhaps I don't wish to talk to you."

Her cheeks had pinked again—it made her even more devastatingly appealing. He gazed in mute admiration.

"Tell me what happened, at least," he managed.

"Very well, since I can see I won't be easily rid of you. Our carriage wheel got stuck in a rut and it took an age to free it. It turns out that if you dig a hole in the King's highway in order to release a vehicle, you're obliged to fill it back in again, and make it better than it was before."

"You got stuck in a rut?" It was fortunate that they'd not been hurt—he was justified in worrying.

"There was a big jolt, and the carriage creaked in protest, but it wasn't damaged. The horses were rather upset at being pulled up so short, but Coachman is very skilled—he calmed them immediately. It was the digging that took the time."

"I am glad neither you nor Miss Bellamy suffered any harm." He was more relieved than she could possibly imagine. He took a deep breath. "Now, to the matter in hand—that of our marriage. I thought you'd agreed to it until the issue of the child came up. I cannot, I *will* not allow that barrier to stand between us—there must be a solution. I have the germ of an idea already, but I need to examine the practicalities. I have, at least, bought us some time, by disposing of Mr. Bilson. Should he decide to contest your occupation of this house, he'll fail. I know the best lawyers in the land." It was convenient, on occasion, to be well-connected.

"You make free with the word 'us', sir. You lied to Thomas about being my fiancé—he'll find out the truth soon enough, and then there'll be trouble. You don't know him as I do."

He moved closer, silently begging her to have some faith in him. "If the only reason for avoiding wedlock is the issue of the child, then I'm grateful. It is an obstacle that can be surmounted." Hopefully, there was nothing else that had turned her against him. He couldn't bear to lose her now.

She glanced away. "A son of ours would be heir to your earldom. How can I ask you to give him up so soon? You've already lost one child—a loss that must have hurt you deeply."

"It did. It still does. I'm glad that you think me human, at the very least." Indeed—she knew *exactly* how human he was. He had spent an entire night proving it to her.

The room turned unaccountably warm. He moved across to the window and gazed out at the darkening sky.

"You'll like Brampton Hall. I'll give you *carte blanche* to decorate it however you wish. It's bigger than this house, and the rooms are arranged differently—they are pleasantly light and airy. You must visit the place with me as soon as possible. You can re-decorate the townhouse too, although you may have to battle my reprobate brother, who uses it more than I do."

"Is he truly a reprobate?" She sounded anxious.

"Indeed. But I still care for him—I'm human, as I said, and am perfectly capable of family feeling. My sibling is the Honorable Roland

Chetwynd, Master of No-Useful-Skills-at-All. Except those of being charming and persuasive. You'll like him." *Women usually did.*

He heard the soft rustle of taffeta and knew Araminta had come to stand close behind him. His body rippled with excitement, but he repressed the urge to spin around and embrace her.

"You're far too sure of everything, sir. We made a business arrangement, not a legal one, so there is no reason to adhere to it. Especially if one of us will have to make so great a sacrifice."

That was too much to bear. He turned and grasped her by the shoulders.

"How can you speak of sacrifice, after the night we spent together? Did that mean nothing to you? I'll have you know that I'm a gentleman, not a despoiler of virgins. I mean, I know you are no virgin—what I mean is, that you have been married. Oh, dash it—you know what I mean!"

He was gabbling like a love-struck youth. It must be her closeness and the heady delight of touching her. It was time to rein in his emotions—he couldn't afford to make a mull of this.

"I don't misunderstand you, Leo." Her expression was grave. "And I can tell there is more to you than I first imagined. But you're a very stubborn, determined man. Even if we *could* resolve our current problems, would our union be happy? I've suffered too much under the rule of my late husband and would struggle with being a wife again. I've thought about it long and hard on the journey here, and have decided to go with my original plan, to adopt a baby and pass it off as my own. I mean to disappear to some remote seaside place for my health, then return with a newborn—"

She paused and frowned up at him, a storm brewing in her hazel eyes. "At least, that was my intention before you informed Mr. Bilson that you were engaged to me. By meddling in my affairs, you've spoiled everything. It's unforgivable."

His fingers gripped harder as if by holding her, he could make her understand. She had no idea what she was doing—she needed a husband to protect her from the vultures that were circling. And not just any husband. *Him.*

"There's one significant difference between your late husband and myself. *He* didn't love you."

Her hands clung to his elbows and for the first time since she'd entered the room, she met his gaze fully. Her eyes were wide and moist, and her lower lip trembled. It was all he could do not to pull her into his embrace and kiss her until they were both gasping for breath.

Her eyes searched his face. "You love me?" Her voice was a mere whisper, sending delicious shivers across his skin.

"Yes. I believe I do. I'm besotted. Does that make a difference?" He felt dizzy, but whether it was from elation or fear, he couldn't tell.

"Yes. It makes all the difference in the world."

Chapter Twelve

Araminta was so deeply engrossed in the glorious rediscovery of Leo's lips that she ignored the clatter of hooves in the courtyard outside. So, apparently, did he, for he pulled her against him and immediately took mastery of her body, igniting flames of desire wherever his hands touched her. It was thus most fortunate that the next person to arrive at the parlor knocked on the door and waited.

With a gasp, Araminta flung herself away from Leo, tucked her hair into place and smoothed down her dress.

"Leo—take that foolish grin off your face. Everyone will know what we've been doing!"

His eyes shone so brightly that she was tempted to tell the visitor to come back later while she explored this fascinating man further. This was the first time she'd seen the touch of blue in his eyes, like the promise of summer. Her heart fluttered, and her voice sounded strangled when she called, "Come in!"

Mrs. Aldridge entered. She glanced at the earl, gave him a brief curtsy, and informed them both that there was a gentleman in the hallway. "He says he is the Honorable Roland Chetwynd and is enquiring after yourself, your lordship."

Araminta exchanged glances with Leo. His brother had followed him to Forty Court—this could not augur well.

"With your permission?" Leo sought Araminta's gaze. He looked grim—he must be thinking the same thing.

She nodded. "Of course, he can be shown in."

"Don't be alarmed, my love. I'm used to dealing with Roland. He's probably here about some mess in which he's become embroiled that has nothing to do with you or me."

The next moment, a tall, blue-eyed, golden-haired Adonis strode into the room. Araminta stared at him in amazement. He was so like Leo, and yet totally *unlike* him. He was a man who could easily break a young girl's heart. Thankfully, her own was now accounted for. *It was?*

The young man looked to be in excellent spirits. It must be *good* news, after all.

"Araminta, allow me to introduce to you the not-at-all-honorable Roland Chetwynd, my scapegrace brother. Roland—this is Lady Lamb. I beg you to be on your best behavior in this house, as I won't have her opinion of me, or my family, tarnished in any way."

At that moment, Belinda swept into the room, announcing that tea was on its way. She fetched up short as soon as she laid eyes on Roland.

A shiver of alarm trickled down Araminta's back. She glanced helplessly at Leo but received a reassuring smile in return.

"I'm delighted to meet you, Lady Lamb." Roland came forward with an outstretched hand. "My brother has told me so much about you."

She sincerely hoped he *hadn't!* It was a battle to retain her composure. "Mr. Chetwynd. This is my sister, Miss Bellamy."

Roland stared in open appreciation, then frowned. "Bellamy. Where have I heard that name recently? Oh, I say!"

Leo clapped his brother on the shoulder and motioned him to a chair. "I forbid you to tax your brain with it—I'll explain later. We're just about to have tea—sit down and behave yourself. Miss Bellamy, if I might trouble you for another cup?"

Belinda exited the room, but not without stealing a further covert glance at the handsome Roland. Araminta rolled her eyes. Belinda had sworn off men after her own ruination and the loss of her child. But the way she'd looked at Roland suggested perhaps she was now on the road to recovery. Catching Leo's eye, she mouthed the word "help".

The look he shot back at her promised a great deal more than assistance with keeping his brother away from Belinda. No man had ever made her feel so protected, and yet so exposed at the same time. Her skin erupted in delicious goosebumps.

Only small talk could save her now—that, and a determination not to snag Leo's gaze again.

She turned to Roland. "How very kind of you to visit. I wonder how you knew where to find us?"

Roland sat forward in his chair. "Oh, Leo usually tells me where he's going. And if he doesn't, one of the servants in our London townhouse will know. Since my brother insists on riding everywhere, he always enquires about various inns and hostelries along the route, so he can take a rest or change horses."

Her face heated. She suddenly realized it must have been Roland who'd been Leo's companion on that fateful, incredible night. So, *he* must know what *she*—what *they*—had done! Oh, if only the floor would swallow her up!

"I assume you have ridden here yourself, to be so hot on my heels." Leo was leaning with one elbow on the arm of his chair, a finger across his mouth concealing his smile. His eyes sparkled at his brother.

"It would have taken too long to bring the carriage. I have news that must be imparted immediately."

To Araminta's consternation, Roland then glanced at her. So, he *did* know about their bargain! What would it take to suddenly become invisible?

"A note came for you, Leo. When I saw the seal, I took the liberty of opening it, since I knew its contents would affect us both. No, don't scowl at me—sometimes I have to make decisions without you. I know that I'm no businessman, but I understand the contents full well."

Roland's chest expanded and he lifted his chin, ensuring all eyes were upon him. "Each one of your cargoes of cotton has arrived—safe and sound. You can unmortgage the house, or whatever it was you did to finance the expedition. You can save the orphanage from Pargeter. I thought you needed to know that as soon as possible."

He glanced at Araminta again, and the air was sucked out of her lungs as she realized what was coming next—the demolition of all her hopes.

No. Don't say it. Please, not now. Not yet.

Roland cleared his throat. "Forgive me, Lady Lamb, but I thought my brother ought to know that there's no longer any need for him to marry one of Bessie Dove-Lyon's heiresses."

Before Araminta could respond, Belinda spoke from the doorway where she had suddenly halted. "You mean, there'll be no marriage? There isn't going to be a baby? But I was so hoping for a baby!" Her mouth was wide with shock.

Araminta immediately rose and put her arm around her sister's shoulders. Neither of the gentlemen present could understand Belinda's pain. Well, perhaps Leo could, having suffered himself, but Roland was completely oblivious. He'd risen the instant Belinda entered the room, and now looked thoroughly wretched, even though he must have no idea of the full extent to which his news had upset her.

The maid, Charlotte, bustled in with the tea tray at that point, and the room descended into an awkward silence. As soon as the servant retreated, Leo jumped to his feet and caught his brother by the elbow.

"I told you he was a complete reprobate, didn't I?" He bowed to Araminta and seized her hand. "Before he does any further damage, I shall take him away to the nearest hostelry. When he's calmed down, and I've taught him how *not* to put his foot in it at every turn—if that's even possible—I'll be back."

After bestowing a brief kiss upon the back of Araminta's hand, he bade Belinda farewell and hustled his brother out of the room.

The Honorable Roland barely had time to say to utter the words "I say," and "lovely to meet you ladies" before being swept from view. Araminta heard Leo's furious command, "Get your hat and coat, you complete idiot!" before the slam of the front door announced their departure.

Dazed, she drifted across to the window and watched as a fine chestnut stallion was brought around from the stables. Mr. Chetwynd's mount hadn't even made it that far, but the groom relinquished it to him with more deference than he deserved.

Belinda joined her at the window. "They are leaving already? Was it something we said?"

"No. It was something the Mr. Chetwynd said."

She must pull herself together. Belinda was troubled—it was time to put her fear aside and comfort her sister.

"Come, my dear." It took every sinew of her being to appear calm. Just when they'd been so close to an understanding, a solution! Would either gentleman ever come back, now they had no need?

"I'm sure we have done no harm," she managed, her voice sounding stronger. "All the gentlemen need is a conversation in private, as gentlemen always do when there are business matters to discuss. They don't wish to confound or bore the ladies with such things—even though some of us are perfectly capable. Never mind—I'm certain they'll let us know the outcome, should it affect *us* in any way. In the meantime, how long ago was breakfast? Are you not famished? We should eat."

"I'll go and find Cook, shall I, and hope she has something in the larder? We didn't give her much notice, did we? There's bound to be some preserves in the cellar, and smoked ham or some such—I'll help her look."

Belinda was happily distracted. For now, at any rate.

Araminta turned her back on the window and the tempting sight of Leo cantering away on his stallion. It was astonishing how empty the house felt without him in it—he had as much presence as Horatio once had, but she responded to Leo's in a very different way.

She smoothed down her skirts. There was luggage to unpack, and gowns that needed to be taken out and aired. Orders needed to be given, rooms must be prepared. Only a maniacal burst of activity would keep her going, would quell the gnawing doubt inside that threatened to overwhelm her.

If what Mr. Chetwynd had said was true, there was no reason why she should ever see Leo again.

Chapter Thirteen

Luncheon was a solemn affair, despite Araminta's attempts at gaiety. The dining room had grown ever darker as they ate, and before long, the sound of rain slashing against the windows could be heard.

Belinda glanced up, resting her fork on her plate. "Is it raining? The gentlemen won't come back if it's raining, will they?"

Araminta pushed a piece of smoked ham around on her plate. She knew she ought to eat, but her body was in such turmoil, she was afraid a single bite could choke her. Her thoughts had been running along the same lines as Belinda's. Why *would* the gentlemen return? Leo's business interests lay in London, as did his brother's—if, indeed, he had any. His personal interests lay in London, at any rate, and doubtless many of them revolved around the Lyon's Den and its clientele. So, as soon as the rain stopped, the men would return to Town.

"It's probably no more than an April shower. It will soon be done with. Then I expect they'll head back to London."

"But it must dry up properly before they can ride that far—the horses won't like splashing around in puddles. And they'll need to rest them, won't they? Both have been ridden many miles today, so they should be stabled here. We have plenty of room."

Araminta sighed. Wasn't her pain bad enough, without Belinda inadvertently making it worse with her false hope? Ah! If only Leo's brother hadn't made his entrance at that moment! What might have happened between herself and Leo? She suspected she knew—and he must have felt it too, or he wouldn't have admitted his feelings.

She pressed her fingers against her forehead. How much could she trust an unintended declaration of love, especially after so short a time? Leo could easily have been pretending—he could have turned on the charm, he could have made an extra effort in the bedchamber to ensure he'd be marrying into money.

But now, he no longer needed to. And now, he was gone.

She rose and pushed away from the table, desperate to be alone with her thoughts. "I'm going to make sure the carriage horses have been groomed and fed properly. No—you stay here and finish your meal, Belinda. I don't want you going out in the rain—remember that terrible cold on the chest you caught the year before last?"

Belinda nodded glumly. "I remember. Lord Lamb had something similar to that, didn't he? But it wouldn't have killed him had he not abused his liver all his life."

"Don't say that to anyone else!" Araminta was horrified that Belinda had remembered her bitter, unsympathetic response when word reached them of Horatio's death.

It was the truth, all the same, and had been the medical prognosis during Horatio's last illness. However, the utterance of those words in front of Belinda had *not* been Araminta's finest moment. She had just been so shocked, *so angry,* that her husband had abandoned everyone to their fate simply because he couldn't curb his appetite for alcohol.

She was a terrible person. Maybe she *deserved* to be abandoned. The only other human being who cared for her, who needed her, was Belinda, and that was what kept her going.

Heaven help her—she was about to break down in front of Belinda! This would *not* do. She seized a hooded cloak, shoved her feet into her galoshes, and escaped outside as the tears started to fall. She knew that she was headed for a spell of self-pity and couldn't bear for anyone else to witness it. To the outside world, she must appear strong even though inside she was breaking apart.

The rain fell less heavily and had changed to a fine drizzle that settled on one's clothes and threatened to drench them in no time, but she didn't care. Turning her back on the house, she hurried through the herb garden and out toward the orchard where blossoms were already beginning to form. Next to that was the walled garden, completely enclosed by ancient high brick walls that shut out the external world.

Rain ran down her face, mingling with her tears as she lifted the latch on the solid wooden door, hurried through the archway, and let the gate swing closed behind her.

At the back of the garden was an ancient platform, from which Horatio's ancestors would have gazed down with pleasure at the complicated knot of low box hedges and the maze of flower beds and graveled paths. There was an arbor, too, that had once been covered in entwined climbing roses, creating a scented summer paradise.

Not long into their marriage, Horatio, despite her objections, had had the roses destroyed, and the arbor roofed over as a place for the gardeners to take shelter. Why could he not have built them a greenhouse to shelter in? Ah, but that would have pleased her, and of course, he couldn't be guilty of *that*.

Having climbed the steps, Araminta negotiated the slippery platform, then took refuge in the arbor. The wind threw the fine rain like a curtain across the front of the structure, and for a moment, she felt as if she were now completely separate from reality, in both body and soul.

The grim truth of what had happened to her, and what she must do, was temporarily thrust aside. There was nothing but her, and the buffeting rain that would make life spring anew in the garden. She gazed out, unseeing, while the cold crept into her limbs, and her tears fell with the rain until she felt drained, empty, numb to all feeling.

The click of the garden gate set her heart thumping. Who was invading her treasured privacy? Was it one of the gardeners, or somebody from the house coming to find her? No, for the figure striding toward her in his billowing riding coat was too tall and erect to be any of them. She pressed her palm to her heart as if she could will it back to a normal rhythm. But she could not. The man heading for her with quiet determination, the rain dripping from his dark hair, was Leo.

"What are you doing out here? You're soaked!" His body filled the entrance to the arbor, shutting out what little light there was. His tone was angry. Before she could respond that she had every right to do as she wished, he'd folded her in his arms and pressed her against his chest.

"You foolish wench." He gazed down at her. "You've been weeping. Not because of me, I hope. I didn't mean to frighten you by leaving, but I had to deal with that accursed Roland. He's disobligingly good at putting his foot in it at the worst possible moment."

She couldn't speak. All she knew was that Leo was holding her and that she could hear the sturdy but rapid beat of his heart against her cheek. This felt like *home*. More than any place she'd ever been before.

"Please—let me reassure you that I have no intention of reneging on our bargain. It was made in good faith."

There was still hope then—this was a man whose word one could trust. But was this a man one might come to love?

"Do you think that having found you, I have any intention of letting you go? I know the circumstances of our coming together are most unusual, but I can't imagine finding happiness with any other woman. I truly love you, Araminta Lamb. If you're willing to be my wife, I hope you'll be happy to be the mistress of Brampton Hall. I'll still do my utmost to ensure Forty Court doesn't fall into the hands of your late husband's rapacious relations, however, as it is rightly and justifiably yours."

He pushed her damp hair from her forehead and kissed her on the bridge of her nose. Her heart swelled.

"I need you more than anything I've ever needed before in my life—so much so that I frighten myself. What frightens me still more is that you might cast me off. Please, if you don't believe my words, feel the beat of my heart. I have more to say, but I'm at risk of babbling and making an utter fool of myself. Which is the very last thing I want to do in front of you, my most precious, my most beloved Araminta."

Her fingers gripped his damp lapels, and she pressed her face against the hard muscles of his chest, relishing the strength she found there. It was so easy to be with him like this, their bodies pressed together, their hearts beating wildly, madly, and their souls in accord.

"Kiss me first. Then you can tell me whatever else you need to say."

She heard the smile in his voice. "It would be churlish of me to refuse you, under the circumstances."

As he bent his head to kiss her, she caught a glimpse of that smile, and all uncertainty fled, to be replaced by a glowing warmth that rapidly burgeoned into the heat of desire. When he eased away from her, she gave a soft mew of disappointment.

"What's the matter?" Surely, she hadn't been too eager in her response? He needed to know how she felt.

"I must tell you the rest of it. So that you know you have a choice, and that I won't crush or coerce you like your first husband. I've thought of a way for you to remain at Forty Court if you prefer to. *And* a way to prevent us from losing contact with our firstborn, if Forty Court remains in your hands. I appreciate that the place is Belinda's home, and I imagine it would be best for her to stay here."

"You don't think she needs to go into an asylum? She doesn't behave like other young women. You haven't seen her in one of her fits."

He looked shocked. "Of course, she mustn't go to an asylum! If you're worried, we'll take medical advice. Though I must say—I've met many fellows who thought themselves sane who were far more worrying than Miss Bellamy."

It all sounded so easy—too easy. But as Araminta had discovered, Leo was a determined man. If it could be achieved, he would find a way.

"And our child?" She quivered at the thought of conceiving a child with him.

"I'll explain all that later." She could feel the excitement trembling through him—he was evidently feeling very pleased with himself. Well, she wouldn't quarrel about that—she was pleased with him, too. More than she could ever have imagined.

"Come now." He took her hand and chafed it between his own. "We must go inside. There are things to do—I have to arrange a special license so we can be married right away. And it would be disastrous should either of us catch a chill and have to postpone our wedding. However, I insist on stealing another kiss before we go in."

Standing wrapped in his embrace, Araminta could feel no chill, no rain. There was nothing to fear because, with him by her side, all obstacles could be overcome. Nothing mattered but her and Leo, their two hearts beating as one. And with love to unite them, her only tears from now on would be tears of joy.

EPILOGUE

Two months later

THE CHANDELIERS BURNED bright, reflecting their golden light onto the dancers down below. The sound of laughter, both male and female, filled the air, gladdening Araminta's heart as she gazed down from the balcony in the Lyon's Den.

But nothing filled her heart with more joy than the upright, raven-haired man standing next to her. Her husband. Leo.

"I suppose we should go down and join the scandalous throng, Lady Aylsham." Leo grinned at her. As it always did, his smile sent arrows of heat shafting along her spine.

"It's a charitable event, I suppose, so mingling with the daredevil men and misfit ladies who are wont to visit the Lyon's Den won't harm our reputation, my lord."

He glanced up. "No exotic women swinging from the ceiling tonight, I see."

Araminta remembered how she'd been clad the last time she'd stood on this balcony, recalling vividly the feeling that had swamped her when she'd gazed at the mysterious, masked stranger below. Leo.

She'd eventually chosen him for her bedmate—and she would never regret it.

He took her hand and kissed it. "Speaking of charitable actions, I never did find out who sent that large donation shortly after we met. I was so certain it was you, and that you were just trying to sweeten me up so you could take one of the foundlings."

It was decidedly puzzling. Particularly since the amount the Foundlings' Hospital had received was exactly half of what she'd given to Mrs. Dove-Lyon in payment for finding her a husband.

As if conjured up by her thoughts, the proprietress of the Lyon's Den came softly through the adjoining doorway and stood beside them.

"I trust you're enjoying your evening, Lord and Lady Aylsham? Also, I hope that you'll shortly be joining us below."

Araminta glanced at Leo, and he nodded. "We're just making the most of a few more moments alone before we join the mob."

Mrs. Dove-Lyon chuckled behind her veil. "I couldn't help but overhear your conversation. I confess—it was I who made that donation. After Lady Aylsham—Lady Lamb as was—had acquainted me with her circumstances, I decided my gesture, particularly if made anonymously, would intrigue you, my lord. You'd assume the money had come from *her* and would seek her out to admonish her."

Leo inclined his head toward her. "Forgive me, but I don't think I'm *that* vindictive."

Mrs. Dove-Lyon interrupted him. "In my experience," she said, sounding not unlike a haughty schoolmistress, "those who care deeply enough about something to argue over it usually have more in common than they know. A heated disagreement arouses the passions and can fan a spark to become a flame."

She paused, letting her words sink in, then added, "Alternatively, Lord Aylsham would recognize the value of such generous donations, and would therefore be more amenable to the idea of marrying an heiress. Or so Mr. Roland Chetwynd encouraged me to believe."

Leo's breath hissed out between his teeth. "That scheming brother of mine!"

Mrs. Dove-Lyon waved a hand. "The scheming was all mine—your brother was merely an unwitting instrument. Pray, do not blame him. Anyway, we're all happy with the outcome, are we not?"

Squeezing her hand, Leo gazed into Araminta's eyes. As he looked at her, she forgot that they were in a public place, forgot they had company, and lost herself in the heady pleasure of his adoration.

A discreet cough from Mrs. Dove-Lyon burst the bubble. "I understand there was a difficulty regarding the first child of your marriage—it was to be taken away, I gather. Has that potential stumbling block been overcome?"

"Indeed, it has." Leo had worked everything out so cleverly—his intelligence, and his willingness to make sacrifices for her, made her want to share her pride in him with all the world.

"My first husband's will stated that any surviving heir should be given into fosterage shortly after birth. The child would thus be taken away from me and become estranged, which was no doubt what the late Lord Lamb intended, as he always made it abundantly clear how disappointed he was in me. He had no faith in my capabilities as a mother or as the manager of an estate. However, the will never specified what *form* the fostering should take. Therefore, a foundlings' hospital or an orphanage home would meet the terms adequately."

She allowed herself a beam of pleasure as a frisson of excitement thrilled through her. *Not yet.* She wanted to hug her delicious secret to herself just a little longer. And it was something that should only be divulged in private.

"When Lord Aylsham came to my home, he conceived the idea of transferring the Lady Aylsham Home for foundling children to Forty Court. London expands northward at such a pace, there will soon be plenty of employment opportunities closer to home. Brampton Hall can be given into Roland Chetwynd's care."

"Into his *well-supervised* care," Leo amended.

"Of course. Leo discussed the possibilities of adapting Forty Court so we could share it with the foundlings—we would live there too, alongside my sister Belinda."

Leo's blue eyes caught the sparkle of the chandeliers. "Not forgetting that I made sensible use of the surveyor and valuer my wife's despicable cousin had already invited to view the place."

"Indeed. Anyway, the new arrangement would mean we could see our child at least once a day and have a say in how it was brought up."

"As best we can without making the other children jealous," Leo reminded her.

"They'd never be jealous, so long as you give them the same attention you always have." She laid her hand over his, where it rested on the balcony rail. "I don't deserve a husband as generous, as caring, as you."

"You deserve far better, but I'll have to do for now." His grin sent tingles coursing across her skin.

Another polite cough from Mrs. Dove-Lyon brought Araminta back to earth. Ah, if only she'd remove her veil so she could see the woman whose machinations had resulted in such a splendid outcome! But Araminta had no right to complain about veils, having deliberately—and no doubt, foolishly—originally concealed her identity from Leo.

"I couldn't be more pleased for the pair of you. I'm also incredibly proud of having engineered this match, despite both of you proving to be difficult subjects. But love is blind, as they say, until someone like myself gives people the eyes to see. Anyway—I wanted to give you a gift. Call it a belated wedding gift, if you wish."

"There's no need, madam. You have already done enough."

Araminta entwined her fingers with Leo's and nodded her agreement. It would be embarrassing to receive a gift from a woman she'd paid to find her a husband.

"I don't think you'll want to refuse it when you see what it is." Mrs. Dove-Lyon's gesture encompassed the hall below.

"I don't understand." Leo frowned.

"I led you to believe that this fundraising ball is for one of my veterans' charities. It is not. The proceeds from the tickets, and whatever the House wins at the tables later, are in aid of the Lady Aylsham Foundlings' Hospital. I didn't know when I planned this that the hospital's location would be changing, but I'm sure you'll find the money useful in organizing the removals."

Araminta gasped. They didn't really need the money anymore, but such a grand gesture could not be refused.

"That's most generous of you, Mrs. Dove-Lyon." Leo bowed to their hostess. "Anything that will smooth the transition from Clerkenwell to the children's new home in the country is much appreciated. We've decided to make the new establishment completely self-sustaining—there will no longer be any subscribers or any Board of Trustees. No one will ever again think of the institution as an asset or of making a profit from the foundlings' plight. Well, I suppose that grasping Pargeter might just turn a profit now he's bought the place. However, I suspect he'll have more difficulty demolishing the buildings than he'd like—Mama ensured they were solidly constructed. It'll be several years before his new warehouses bring him any profit. I, for one, won't be selling any of *my* cotton in them."

"It seems everything has turned out as it should."

"Thanks to you, madam. I apologize if I ever misunderstood what goes on here. Should any of our acquaintance take the name of the Lyon's Den in vain, we'll be the first to correct them. Won't we, my darling?"

The atmosphere warmed, and Mrs. Dove-Lyon must have sensed her presence was no longer required, for the next instant, she was gone.

Leo snaked an arm around Araminta's waist, and she snuggled into his side.

"That was unexpected, was it not, my sweet? I thought our hostess was a hardheaded businesswoman, but it turns out she conceals a soft heart."

Araminta nodded her agreement. "For all we know, she may have been an orphan herself or has lost a child. She's such a mysterious person that I doubt we'll ever discover what happened in her past, or what drives her now."

Leo's fingers stroked Araminta's flank, igniting a blaze of sumptuous sensations. "I can't deny that this is a bizarre place, despite all the good it dispenses. There's a high-class bordello upstairs, gambling dens for both men and women, a peculiar cage for the exchange of money, and people who seem to be trapped in there every time we visit. Not to mention the so-called Abacus Woman who deals with all the money. There are passing peculiarities as well, like that scantily-clad swinging woman who dispensed me my winning ticket. The web woven by the woman at the heart of all this is so complex, I daresay no one will ever unravel its strands. This is exactly the place for those who do not belong in the outside world to get work—they find shelter here, and respite from their troubles, while the customers find pleasure and diversion."

"You see and absorb a good deal more than you let on." Her husband never failed to surprise her. Indeed, she suspected she would never be able to plumb the depths of the man—but that was of no matter. She loved everything about him, both what she knew and what she had yet to discover.

Her love for him ran deep. Her love for him was thorough. Her love was unconditional.

"I suppose we'd had better go down and foot it with the others. I don't want to trust the impressionable Miss Bellamy to my brother's care for any longer than is necessary."

True. It wasn't wise to leave Belinda for long in a gathering such as this. "I just wanted to come up here again for a moment, because this spot has such significance for both of us."

He tilted his head at her. "I would have thought the tapestried room without windows held more of *that*."

His feral grin held an invitation her body couldn't ignore. He tipped his head subtly in the direction of the aforementioned room.

She fluttered her fan at him. "You just said that we couldn't leave Belinda in Roland's care any longer than need be. We must go down, husband, and tread a measure with them. And then, perhaps, we might return to the townhouse."

Leo's handsome face assumed an exaggerated expression of disappointment. "We were talking about heirs earlier. Are you sure you don't want to make another attempt at ensuring that we have one? After all, it would be a very significant place for him to be conceived."

Araminta's flush heated her face, spread across her chest, and suffused her entire body. She glanced at the crowd below—no one was paying them any attention. Now might be as good a moment as any to slip away.

"Not that I wish to change our nighttime arrangements, my lord, but there's no need to worry about the production of an heir." She paused and leaned in closer to him. "I'm already increasing."

He stared at her, nonplussed. After a moment, he found his voice. "I beg your pardon?"

Damn the man! Must she spell it out for him? "What I'm saying is, that I'm now carrying your child."

He sucked in a breath, let out a very un-earl-like whoop of pleasure, and seized her in his arms.

She pushed against him, but her struggles were useless. "Please stop. People will stare."

"I don't give a cuss about people. This is between you and me, wife. You made me the happiest man on Earth when I married you. I didn't think it was possible to be happier—but you've just shown me that it is. I thank all the gods that I met you, that Fate brought us together and Fortune kept us so."

The joy on his face was overwhelming. She had never loved him more than she did at that moment.

"Not just fate, husband," she murmured, through the mist of joyful tears. "Don't forget that we owe a great deal to the Lyon's Den."

"I shan't forget it." He took her hand and pressed it to his lips, then held onto it as if he could never let her go.

After what seemed an eternity, he sighed. "I suppose we'd better go and share the good news with the rest of the family."

"I suppose we better had."

She took his arm, thrust her shoulders back, and held her head high. Lady Lamb had been treated like a downtrodden servant. But now, she'd found her perfect partner, her dashing nobleman, and it didn't matter what life threw at her from now on—she would never suffer.

Because the Lamb had surrendered to the Lyon, and it was the best decision she had ever made.

The End

About the Author

Elizabeth Keysian is an international bestselling author of heart-pounding Regency romances, set mostly in the West of England. She is working on a fresh series for Dragonblade Publishing called Trysts and Treachery, which is set in the Tudor era. Though primarily a writer of romance, she loves to put a bit of mystery, adventure, and suspense into her stories, and refuses to let her characters take themselves too seriously.

Elizabeth likes to write from experience, not easy when her works range from the medieval to the Victorian eras. However, her passion for re-enactment has helped, as have the many years she spent working in museums and British archaeology. If you find some detail in her work you've never come across before, you can bet she either dug it up, quite literally, or found it on a museum shelf.

Social media/web links

Newsletter
eepurl.com/cxe369

Amazon page
amazon.com/Elizabeth-Keysian/e/B06VVL9JMB

Twitter
twitter.com/EKeysian

Facebook
m.facebook.com/LizKeysian

BookBub
bookbub.com/profile/elizabeth-keysian

Website
elizabethkeysian.com

Made in United States
North Haven, CT
07 June 2023